I0567228

W.W. JACOBS – THE SHORT STORIES
VOLUME 5

William Wymark Jacobs was born on September 8th, 1863 in the Wapping district of London, England. Jacobs grew up near the docks, where his father was a wharf manager. The docks and river side would be a constant theme of his writing in years to come.

Although surrounded by poverty, he received a formal education in London, first at a private prep school and later at the Birkbeck Literary and Scientific Institute.

His working life began with a less than exciting clerical position at the Post Office Savings Bank. Jacobs put his imagination to good use writing short stories, sketches and articles, many for the Post Office house publication "Blackfriars Magazine."

In 1896 Jacobs published Many Cargoes, a selection of sea-faring yarns, which established him as a popular writer with a knack for authentic dialogue and trick endings.

A year later he published a novelette, The Skipper's Wooing, and in 1898 another collection of short stories; Sea Urchins. These works painted vivid pictures of dockland and seafaring London full of colourful characters.

By 1899, Jacobs was able to quit the post office and write full-time.

He married the noted suffragist Agnes Eleanor Williams (who had been jailed for her protest activities) in 1900. They set up households both in Loughton, Essex and in central London.

The publication in 1902 of At Sunwich Port and Dialstone Lane, in 1904, cemented Jacobs' reputation as one of the leading British authors of the new century.

There followed a string of further successful publications, including Captain's All (1905), Night Watches (1914), The Castaways (1916), and Sea Whispers (1926).

Though Jacobs would create little in the way of new work after 1911, he still wrote and was recognized as a leading humorist, ranked alongside such writers as P. G. Wodehouse.

William Wymark Jacobs died in a North London nursing home in Hornsey Lane, Islington on September 1st, 1943.

Index of Contents

THE DISBURSEMENT SHEET

The old man was dead, and his son Edward reigned in his stead. The old man had risen from a humble position in life; his rule was easy, and his manner of conducting business eminently approved of by the rough old seamen who sailed his small craft round the coast, and by that sharp clerk Simmons, on whose discovery the old man was wont, at times, to hug himself in secret. The proceedings, when one of his skippers came home from a voyage, were severely simple. The skipper would produce a bag, and, emptying it upon the table, give an account of his voyage; whenever he came to an expenditure, raking the sum out of the heap, until, at length, the cash was divided into two portions, one of which went to the owner, the other to the skipper.

But other men other manners. The books of the inimitable Simmons being overhauled, revealed the startling fact that they were kept by single entry; in addition to which, a series of dots and dashes appeared against the figures forming a code, the only key to which was locked up somewhere in Simmons's interior.

"It's a wonder the firm hasn't gone bankrupt long ago," said the new governor, after the clerk had explained the meaning of various signs and wonders. "What does this starfish against the entry mean?"

"It isn't a starfish, sir," said Simmons; "it means that one bag of sugar got wetted a little; then, if the consignees notice it, we shall know we have got to allow for it."

"A pretty way of doing business, upon my word. It'll all have to be altered," said the other. "I must have new offices too; this dingy little hole is enough to frighten people away."

The conversation was interrupted by the entrance of Captain Fazackerly, of the schooner Sarah Ann, who, having just brought up in the river, had hastened to the office to report.

"Mornin', sir," said the captain respectfully; "I'm glad to see you here, sir, but the office don't seem real-like without your father sitting in it. He was a good master, and we're all sorry to lose him."

"You're very good," said the new master somewhat awkwardly.

"I expect it'll take some time for you to get into the way of it," said the captain, with a view to giving the conversation a more cheerful turn.

"I expect it will," said the new master, thinking of the starfish.

"It's a mercy Simmons wasn't took too," said the captain, shaking his head. "As it is, he's spared; he'll be able to teach you. There ain't"—he lowered his voice, not wishing to make Simmons unduly proud—"there ain't a smarter clerk in all Liverpool than wot he is."

"I'm glad to hear it," said the new master, regarding the old man with raised eyebrows, as he extricated a plethoric-looking canvas bag from his jacket pocket and dropped it with a musical crash on the chipped office table. His eyebrows went still higher, as the old man unfastened the string, and emptying the contents on to the table, knitted his brows into reflective wrinkles, and began to debit the firm with all the liabilities of a slow but tenacious memory.

"Oh, come," said the owner sharply, as the old man lovingly hooked out the sum of five-and sixpence as a first instalment, "this won't do, cap'n."

"Wot won't do, Mas'r Edward?" inquired the old man in surprise.

"Why, this way of doing business," said the other. "It's not businesslike at all, you know."

"Well, it's the way me an' your pore old father has done it this last thirty year," said the skipper, "an' I'm sure I've never knowingly cheated him out of a ha'penny; and a better man o' business than your father never breathed."

"Yes; well, I'm going to do things a bit differently," said the new master. "You must give me a proper disbursement sheet, cap'n, if you please."

"And what may that be?" inquired Captain Fazackerly, as with great slowness he gathered up the money and replaced it in the bag; "I never heard of it afore."

"Well, I haven't got time to teach you bookkeeping," said the other, somewhat nettled at the old man's manner. "Can't you get some of your brother captains to show you? Some deep-sea man would be sure to know."

"I'll see what I can do, sir," said the skipper slowly, as he turned towards the door. "My word was always good enough for your father."

In a moody, indignant frame of mind he stuck his hands furiously in his trousers' pockets, and passed heavily through the swing-doors. At other times he had been wont to take a genial, if heavy interest in passing events; but, in this instance, he plodded on, dwelling darkly upon his grievance, until he reached, by the mere force of habit, a certain favourite tavern. He pulled up sharply, and, as a mere matter of duty and custom, and not because he wanted it, went in and ordered a glass of gin.

He drank three, and was so hazy in his replies to the young lady behind the bar, usually a prime favourite, that she took offence, and availing herself, for private reasons, of a public weapon, coldly declined to serve him with a fourth.

"Wot?" said the astounded Fazackerly, coming out of his haze.

"You've had enough!" said the girl firmly. "You get aboard again, and mind how you do so."

The skipper gazed at her for a moment in open-mouthed horror, and then jamming his hat firmly over his brows, stumbled out of the door and into the street, where he ran full into the arms of another mariner who was just entering.

"Why, Zacky, my boy," cried the latter, clapping him lustily on the back, "how goes it?"

In broken, indignant accents the other told him.

"You come in with me," said the new-comer.

"I'll never enter that pub again," said the skipper.

"You come in with me," said the master-mind firmly.

Captain Fazackerly hesitated a moment, and then, feeling that he was safe in the hands of the master of a foreign-going barque, followed him into the bar, and from behind his back glared defiantly at his fair foe.

"Two glasses o' gin, my dear," said Captain Tweedie with the slightest possible emphasis.

The girl, who knew her customer, served him without a murmur, deftly avoiding the gaze of ungenerous triumph with which the injured captain favoured her as he raised the cooling beverage to his lips. The glass emptied, he placed it on the counter and sighed despondently.

"There's something up with you, Zacky," said Tweedie, eyeing him closely as he bit the end off a cigar; "you've got something on your mind."

"I've been crool hurt," said his friend in a hard, cold voice. "My word ain't good enough for the new guv'nor; he wants what he calls a disbursement sheet."

"Well, give him one," said Tweedie. "You know what it is, don't you?"

Captain Fazackerly shook his head, and pushing the glasses along the counter nodded for them to be refilled.

"You come aboard with me," said Tweedie after they had emptied them.

Captain Fazackerly, who had a doglike faith in his friend, followed him into the street and on to his barque. In a general way he experienced a social rise when he entered the commodious cabin of that noble craft, and his face grew in importance as his host, after motioning him to a seat, placed a select array of writing materials before him.

"I s'pose I've got to do it," he said slowly.

"Of course you have," said Tweedie, rolling his cigar between his thin lips; "you've got orders to do so, haven't you? We must all obey those above us. What would you do if one of your men refused to obey an order of yours?"

"Hit him in the face," said Captain Fazackerly with simple directness.

"Just so," said Tweedie, who was always ready to impart moral teaching. "And when your governor asks for a disbursement sheet you've got to give him one. Now, then, head that paper—Voyage of the Sarah Ann, 180 tons register, Garston Docks to Limerick."

The captain squared his elbows, and, for a few seconds, nothing was heard but his stertorous breathing and the scratching of the pen; then a muttered execration, and Captain Fazackerly put down his pen with a woebegone air.

"What's the matter?" said Tweedie.

"I've spelt register without the 'd,'" said the other; "that's what comes o' being worried."

"It don't matter," said Tweedie hastily. "Now what about stores? Wait a bit, though; of course ye repaired your side-lamps before starting?"

"Lor', no!" said Captain Fazackerly, staring; "what for? They were all right."

"Ye lie," said Tweedie sternly, "you did! To repairs to side-lamps, ten shillings. Now then, did you paint her this trip?"

"I did," said the other, looking at the last entry in a fascinated fashion.

"Let's see," said Tweedie meditatively—"we'll say five gallons of black varnish at one shilling and threepence a gallon—"

"No, no," said the scribe; "I used gas tar at threepence a gallon."

"Five gallons black varnish, one shilling and threepence a gallon, six-and-threepence," said Tweedie, raising his voice a little; "have you got that down?"

After a prolonged struggle with his feelings the other said he had.

"Twenty-eight pounds black paint at twopence a pound," continued Tweedie.

"Nay, nay," said the skipper; "I allus saves the soot out of the galley for that."

The other captain took his cigar from his lips and gazed severely at his guest.

"Am I dealing with a chimney-sweep or a ship's captain?" he inquired plaintively; "it would simplify matters a bit if I knew."

"Go on, Captain Tweedie," said the other, turning a fine purple colour; "how much did you say it was?"

"Twenty-eight twos equals fifty-six; that's four-and-ninepence," continued Tweedie, his face relaxing to receive the cigar again; "and twenty-eight pounds white lead at twenty-eight shillings a hundredweight—"

"Three penn'orth o' whiting's good enough for me, matey," said Captain Fazackerly, making a stand.

"See here," said Tweedie, "who's making out this disbursement sheet, you or me?"

"You are," said the other.

"Very good then," said his friend; "now don't you interrupt. I don't mind telling you, you must never use rubbish o' that sort in a disbursement sheet. It looks bad for the firm. If any other owners saw that in your old man's sheet he'd never hear the end of it, and he'd never forgive you. That'll be—

what did I say? Seven shillings. And now we come to the voyage. Ye had a tug to give ye a pluck out to the bar?"

"No; we went out with a fair wind," said Captain Fazackerly, toying with his pen.

"Ye lie; ye had a tug out to the bar," repeated Tweedie wearily. "Did ye share the towing?"

"Why, no, I tell 'e—"

"That'll be three pounds then," said Tweedie. "If ye'd shared it it would have been two pound ten. You should always study your owner in these matters, cap'n. Now, what about bad weather? Any repairs to the sails?"

"Ay, we had a lot o' damage," said Fazackerly, laying down his pen; "it took us days to repair 'em. Cost us four pounds. We had to put into Holyhead for shelter."

"Four pounds!" said Tweedie, his voice rising almost to a scream.

"Ay, all that," said Fazackerly very solemnly.

"Look here," said Tweedie in a choked voice. "Blown away fore lower topsail, fore-staysail, and carried away lifts to staysail. To sailmaker for above, eleven pounds eighteen shillings and ten-pence. Then ye say ye put into Holyhead for shelter. Well, here in entering harbour we'll say loss of port anchor and thirty fathoms of chain cable—"

"Man alive," said the overwrought skipper, hitting the table heavily with his fist, "the old anchor's there for him to see."

"To divers for recovering same, and placing on deck, two pound ten," continued Tweedie, raising his voice. "Did you do any damage going into dock at Limerick?"

"More than we've done for years," said Fazackerly, and shaking his head, entered into voluminous details; "total, seven pounds."

"Seven pounds!" said the exasperated Tweedie. "Seven pounds for all that, and your insurance don't begin till twenty-five pounds. Why, damme, you ain't fit to be trusted out with a ship. I firmly b'lieve if you lost her you'd send in a bill for a suit of clothes, and call it square. Now take this down, and larn a business way o' doing things. In entering dock, carried away starboard cathead and started starboard chain plates; held survey of damage done: decided to take off channel bends, renew through bolts, straighten plates and replace same; also to renew cathead and caulk ship's side in wake of plate, six seams, &c. &c. There, now, that looks better. Twenty-seven pounds eighteen and seven-pence halfpenny, and I think, for all that damage, it's a very reasonable bill. Can you remember anything else?"

"You've got a better memory than I have," said his admiring friend. "Wait a bit, though; yes, I had my poor old dog washed overboard."

"Dog!" said the deep-sea man; "we can't put dogs in a disbursement sheet. 'Tain't business."

"My old master would have given me another one, though," grumbled Fazackerly. "I wouldn't ha' parted with that dog for anything. He knew as much as you or me, that dog did. I never knew him to bite an officer, but I don't think there was ever a man came on the ship but what he'd have a bit out of, sooner or later."

"Them sort of dogs do get washed overboard," said Tweedie impatiently.

"Boys he couldn't abear," pursued the other, in tones of tender reminiscence; "the mere sight of a boarding-school of 'em out for a walk would give him hydrophoby almost."

"Just so," said Tweedie. "Ah! there's cork fenders; ye may pick them up floating down the river, or they may come aboard in the night from a craft alongside; they're changeable sort o' things, but in the disbursement sheet they must go, and best quality too, four-and-sixpence each. Anything else?"

"There's the dog," said Fazackerly persistently.

"Copper nails, tenpence," said Tweedie the dictator.

"Haven't bought any for months," said the other, but slowly entering it.

"Well, it ain't exactly right," said Tweedie, shrugging his shoulders, "but you're so set on him going in."

"Him? Who?" asked Captain Fazackerly, staring.

"The dog," said Tweedie; "if he goes in as copper nails, he won't be noticed."

"If he goes in as tenpence, I'm a Dutchman," said the bereaved owner, scoring out the copper nails. "You never knew that dog properly, Tweedie."

"Well, never mind about the dog," said Tweedie; "let's cast the sheet. What do you think it comes to?"

"'Bout thirty pun'," hazarded the other.

"Thirty fiddlesticks," retorted Tweedie; "there you are in black and white—sixty-three pounds eighteen shillings and tenpence ha'penny."

"And is that what Mas'r Edward wants?" inquired Captain Fazackerly, gasping.

"Yes; that's a properly drawn up disbursement sheet," said Tweedie in satisfied tones. "You see how it simplifies matters. The governor can see at a glance how things stand, while, if you trusted to your memory, you might forget something, or else claim something you didn't have."

"I ought to have had them things afore," said Captain Fazackerly, shaking his head solemnly. "I'd ha' been riding in my carriage by now."

"Never ye dream of having another v'y'ge without one," said Tweedie. "I doubt whether it's lawful to render an account without one."

He folded the paper, and handed it to his friend, who, after inspecting it with considerable pride, tucked it carefully away in his breast pocket.

"Take it up in the morning," said Tweedie. "We'll have a bit o' tea down here, and then we'll go round a bit afterwards."

Captain Fazackerly having no objection, they had tea first, and then, accompanied by the first mate, went out to christen the disbursement sheet. The ceremony, which was of great length, was solemnly impressive towards the finish. Captain Tweedie, who possessed a very sensitive, highly-strung nature, finding it necessary to put a licensed victualler out of his own house before it could be completed to his satisfaction.

The one thing which Captain Fazackerly remembered clearly the next morning when he awoke was the disbursement sheet. He propped it against the coffee-pot during breakfast, and read selections to his admiring mate, and after a refreshing toilet, proceeded to the office. Simmons was already there, and before the skipper could get to the purpose of his visit, the head of the firm arrived.

"I've just brought the disbursement sheet you asked for, sir," said the skipper, drawing it from his pocket.

"Ah! you've got it, then," said the new governor, with a gracious smile; "you see it wasn't so much trouble after all."

"I don't mind the trouble, sir," interrupted Captain Fazackerly.

"You see it puts things on a better footing," said the other. "I can see at a glance now how things stand, and Simmons can enter the items straight away into the books of the firm. It's more satisfactory to both of us. Sit down, cap'n."

The captain sat down, his face glowing with this satisfactory recognition of his work.

"I met Cap'n Hargreaves as I was a-coming up," he said; "and I explained to him your ideas on the subject, an' he went straight back, as straight as he could go, to make out his disbursement sheet."

"Ah! we shall soon have things on a better footing now," said the governor, unfolding the paper, while the skipper gazed abstractedly through the small, dirty panes of the office window at the bustle on the quay below.

For a short space there was silence in the office, broken only by the half-audible interjections of the reader. Then he spoke.

"Simmons!" he said sharply.

The old clerk slipped from his stool, and obeying the motions of his employer inspected, in great astonishment, the first disbursement sheet which had ever entered the office. He read through every item in an astonished whisper, and, having finished, followed the governor's example and gazed at the heavy figure by the window.

"Captain Fazackerly," said his employer, at length, breaking a painful silence.

"Sir," said the captain, turning his head a little.

"I've been talking with Simmons about these disbursement sheets," said the owner, somewhat awkwardly; "Simmons is afraid they'll give him a lot of extra trouble."

The captain turned his head a little more, and gazed stolidly at the astonished Simmons.

"A man oughtn't to mind a little extra trouble if the firm wishes it," he said somewhat severely.

"He's afraid it would throw his books out a bit," continued the owner, deftly avoiding the gaze of the injured clerk. "You see, Simmons' book-keeping is of the old-fashioned kind, cap'n, star-fishes and all that kind of thing," he continued, incoherently, as the gaze of Simmons, refusing to be longer avoided, broke the thread of his discourse. "So I think we'll put the paper on the fire, cap'n, and do business in the old way. Have you got the money with you?"

"I have, sir," said Fazackerly, feeling in his pocket, as he mournfully watched his last night's work blazing up the chimney.

"Fire away, then," said the owner, almost cordially.

Captain Fazackerly advanced to the table, and clearing his throat, fixed his eyes in a reflective stare on the opposite wall and commenced:—

"Blown away fore lower topsail, fore-staysail, and carried away lifts to staysail. To sailmaker for above, eleven pounds eighteen shillings and ten-pence," he said, with relish. "Tug out to the bar, three pounds. To twenty-eight pounds black soot, I mean paint—"

DIXON'S RETURN

Talking about eddication, said the night-watchman, thoughtfully, the finest eddication you can give a lad is to send 'im to sea. School is all right up to a certain p'int, but arter that comes the sea. I've been there myself and I know wot I'm talking about. All that I am I owe to 'aving been to sea.

There s a saying that boys will be boys. That's all right till they go to sea, and then they 'ave to be men, and good men too. They get knocked about a bit, o' course, but that's all part o' the eddication, and when they get bigger they pass the eddication they've received on to other boys smaller than wot they are. Arter I'd been at sea a year I spent all my fust time ashore going round and looking for boys wot 'ad knocked me about afore I sailed, and there was only one out o' the whole lot that I wished I 'adn't found.

Most people, o' course, go to sea as boys or else not at all, but I mind one chap as was pretty near thirty years old when 'e started. It's a good many years ago now, and he was landlord of a public-'ouse as used to stand in Wapping, called the Blue Lion.

His mother, wot had 'ad the pub afore 'im, 'ad brought 'im up very quiet and genteel, and when she died 'e went and married a fine, handsome young woman who 'ad got her eye on the pub without thinking much about 'im. I got to know about it through knowing the servant that lived there. A nice, quiet gal she was, and there wasn't much went on that she didn't hear. I've known 'er to cry for hours with the ear-ache, pore gal.

Not caring much for 'er 'usband, and being spoiled by 'im into the bargain, Mrs. Dixon soon began to lead 'im a terrible life. She was always throwing his meekness and mildness up into 'is face, and arter they 'ad been married two or three years he was no more like the landlord o' that public-'ouse than I'm like a lord. Not so much. She used to get into such terrible tempers there was no doing anything with 'er, and for the sake o' peace and quietness he gave way to 'er till 'e got into the habit of it and couldn't break 'imself of it.

They 'adn't been married long afore she 'ad her cousin, Charlie Burge, come in as barman, and a month or two arter that 'is brother Bob, who 'ad been spending a lot o' time looking for work instead o' doing it, came too. They was so comfortable there that their father—a 'ouse-painter by trade—came round to see whether he couldn't paint the Blue Lion up a bit and make 'em look smart, so that they'd get more trade. He was one o' these 'ere fust-class 'ousepainters that can go to sleep on a ladder holding a brush in one hand and a pot o' paint in the other, and by the time he 'ad finished painting the 'ouse it was ready to be done all over agin.

I dare say that George Dixon—that was 'is name—wouldn't ha' minded so much if 'is wife 'ad only been civil, but instead o' that she used to make fun of 'im and order 'im about, and by-and-by the others began to try the same thing. As I said afore, Dixon was a very quiet man, and if there was ever anybody to be put outside Charlie or Bob used to do it. They tried to put me outside once, the two of 'em, but they on'y did it at last by telling me that somebody 'ad gone off and left a pot o' beer standing on the pavement. They was both of 'em fairly strong young chaps with a lot of bounce in 'em, and she used to say to her 'usband wot fine young fellers they was, and wot a pity it was he wasn't like 'em.

Talk like this used to upset George Dixon awful. Having been brought up careful by 'is mother, and keeping a very quiet, respectable 'ouse—I used it myself—he cert'nly was soft, and I remember 'im telling me once that he didn't believe in fighting, and that instead of hitting people you ought to try and persuade them. He was uncommon fond of 'is wife, but at last one day, arter she 'ad made a laughing-stock of 'im in the bar, he up and spoke sharp to her.

"Wot?" ses Mrs. Dixon, 'ardly able to believe her ears.

"Remember who you're speaking to; that's wot I said," ses Dixon.

"'Ow dare you talk to me like that?" screams 'is wife, turning red with rage. "Wot d'ye mean by it?"

"Because you seem to forget who is master 'ere," ses Dixon, in a trembling voice.

"Master?" she ses, firing up. "I'll soon show you who's master. Go out o' my bar; I won't 'ave you in it. D'ye 'ear? Go out of it."

Dixon turned away and began to serve a customer. "D'ye hear wot I say?" ses Mrs. Dixon, stamping 'er foot. "Go out o' my bar. Here, Charlie!"

"Hullo!" ses 'er cousin, who 'ad been standing looking on and grinning.

"Take the master and put 'im into the parlour," ses Mrs. Dixon, "and don't let 'im come out till he's begged my pardon."

"Go on," ses Charlie, brushing up 'is shirt-sleeves; "in you go. You 'ear wot she said."

He caught 'old of George Dixon, who 'ad just turned to the back o' the bar to give a customer change out of 'arf a crown, and ran 'im kicking and struggling into the parlour. George gave 'im a silly little punch in the chest, and got such a bang on the 'ead back that at fust he thought it was knocked off.

When 'e came to 'is senses agin the door leading to the bar was shut, and 'is wife's uncle, who 'ad been asleep in the easy-chair, was finding fault with 'im for waking 'im up.

"Why can't you be quiet and peaceable?" he ses, shaking his 'ead at him. "I've been 'ard at work all the morning thinking wot colour to paint the back-door, and this is the second time I've been woke up since dinner. You're old enough to know better."

"Go and sleep somewhere else, then," ses Dixon. "I don't want you 'ere at all, or your boys neither. Go and give somebody else a treat; I've 'ad enough of the whole pack of you."

He sat down and put 'is feet in the fender, and old Burge, as soon as he 'ad got 'is senses back, went into the bar and complained to 'is niece, and she came into the parlour like a thunderstorm.

"You'll beg my uncle's pardon as well as mine afore you come out o' that room," she said to her 'usband; "mind that."

George Dixon didn't say a word; the shame of it was a'most more than 'e could stand. Then 'e got up to go out o' the parlour and Charlie pushed 'im back agin. Three times he tried, and then 'e stood up and looked at 'is wife.

"I've been a good 'usband to you," he ses; "but there's no satisfying you. You ought to ha' married somebody that would ha' knocked you about, and then you'd ha' been happy. I'm too fond of a quiet life to suit you."

"Are you going to beg my pardon and my uncle's pardon?" ses 'is wife, stamping 'er foot.

"No," ses Dixon; "I am not. I'm surprised at you asking it."

"Well, you don't come out o' this room till you do," ses 'is wife.

"That won't hurt me," ses Dixon. "I couldn't look anybody in the face arter being pushed out o' my own bar."

They kept 'im there all the rest o' the day, and, as 'e was still obstinate when bedtime came, Mrs. Dixon, who wasn't to be beat, brought down some bedclothes and 'ad a bed made up for 'im on the sofa. Some men would ha' 'ad the police in for less than that, but George Dixon 'ad got a great deal o' pride and 'e couldn't bear the shame of it. Instead o' that 'e acted like a fourteen-year-old boy and ran away to sea.

They found 'im gone when they came down in the morning, and the side-door on the latch. He 'ad left a letter for 'is wife on the table, telling 'er wot he 'ad done. Short and sweet it was, and wound up with telling 'er to be careful that her uncle and cousins didn't eat 'er out of house and 'ome.

She got another letter two days arterward, saying that he 'ad shipped as ordinary seaman on an American barque called the *Seabird,* bound for California, and that 'e expected to be away a year, or thereabouts.

"It'll do 'im good," ses old Burge, when Mrs. Dixon read the letter to 'em. "It's a 'ard life is the sea, and he'll appreciate his 'ome when 'e comes back to it agin. He don't know when 'e's well off. It's as comfortable a 'ome as a man could wish to 'ave." It was surprising wot a little difference George Dixon's being away made to the Blue Lion. Nobody seemed to miss 'im much, and things went on just the same as afore he went. Mrs. Dixon was all right with most people, and 'er relations 'ad a very good time of it; old Burge began to put on flesh at such a rate that the sight of a ladder made 'im ill a'most, and Charlie and Bob went about as if the place belonged to 'em.

They 'eard nothing for eight months, and then a letter came for Mrs. Dixon from her 'usband in which he said that 'e had left the *Seabird* after 'aving had a time which made 'im shiver to think of. He said that the men was the roughest of the rough and the officers was worse, and that he 'ad hardly 'ad a day without a blow from one or the other since he'd been aboard. He'd been knocked down with a hand-spike by the second mate, and had 'ad a week in his bunk with a kick given 'im by the boatswain. He said 'e was now on the *Rochester Castle,* bound for Sydney, and he 'oped for better times.

That was all they 'eard for some months, and then they got another letter saying that the men on the *Rochester Castle* was, if anything, worse than those on the Seabird, and that he'd begun to think that running away to sea was diff'rent to wot he'd expected, and that he supposed 'e'd done it too late in life. He sent 'is love to 'is wife and asked 'er as a favour to send Uncle Burge and 'is boys away, as 'e didn't want to find them there when 'e came home, because they was the cause of all his sufferings.

"He don't know 'is best friends," ses old Burge. "'E's got a nasty sperrit I don't like to see."

"I'll 'ave a word with 'im when 'e does come home," ses Bob. "I s'pose he thinks 'imself safe writing letters thousands o' miles away."

The last letter they 'ad came from Auckland, and said that he 'ad shipped on the *Monarch,* bound for the Albert Docks, and he 'oped soon to be at 'ome and managing the Blue Lion, same as in the old happy days afore he was fool enough to go to sea.

That was the very last letter, and some time arterward the *Monarch* was in the missing list, and by-and-by it became known that she 'ad gone down with all hands not long arter leaving New Zealand. The only difference it made at the Blue Lion was that Mrs. Dixon 'ad two of 'er dresses dyed black, and the others wore black neckties for a fortnight and spoke of Dixon as pore George, and said it was a funny world, but they supposed everything was for the best.

It must ha' been pretty near four years since George Dixon 'ad run off to sea when Charlie, who was sitting in the bar one arternoon reading the paper, things being dull, saw a man's head peep through the door for a minute and then disappear. A'most direckly arterward it looked in at another door and then disappeared agin. When it looked in at the third door Charlie 'ad put down 'is paper and was ready for it.

"Who are you looking for?" he ses, rather sharp. "Wot d'ye want? Are you 'aving a game of peepbo, or wot?"

The man coughed and smiled, and then 'e pushed the door open gently and came in, and stood there fingering 'is beard as though 'e didn't know wot to say.

"I've come back, Charlie," he ses at last.

"Wot, George!" ses Charlie, starting. "Why, I didn't know you in that beard. We all thought you was dead, years ago."

"I was pretty nearly, Charlie," ses Dixon, shaking his 'ead. "Ah! I've 'ad a terrible time since I left 'once."

"'You don't seem to ha' made your fortune," ses Charlie, looking down at 'is clothes. "I'd ha' been ashamed to come 'ome like that if it 'ad been me."

"I'm wore out," ses Dixon, leaning agin the bar. "I've got no pride left; it's all been knocked out of me. How's Julia?"

"She's all right," ses Charlie. "Here, Ju—"

"H'sh!" ses Dixon, reaching over the bar and laying his 'and on his arm. "Don't let 'er know too sudden; break it to 'er gently."

"Fiddlesticks!" ses Charlie, throwing his 'and off and calling, "Here, Julia! He's come back."

Mrs. Dixon came running downstairs and into the bar. "Good gracious!" she ses, staring at her 'usband. "Whoever'd ha' thought o' seeing you agin? Where 'ave you sprung from?"

"Ain't you glad to see me, Julia?" ses George Dixon.

"Yes, I s pose so; if you've come back to behave yourself," ses Mrs. Dixon. "What 'ave you got to say for yourself for running away and then writing them letters, telling me to get rid of my relations?"

"That's a long time ago, Julia," ses Dixon, raising the flap in the counter and going into the bar. "I've gone through a great deal o' suffering since then. I've been knocked about till I 'adn't got any feeling left in me; I've been shipwrecked, and I've 'ad to fight for my life with savages."

"Nobody asked you to run away," ses his wife, edging away as he went to put his arm round 'er waist. "You'd better go upstairs and put on some decent clothes."

Dixon looked at 'er for a moment and then he 'ung his 'ead.

"I've been thinking o' you and of seeing you agin every day since I went away, Julia," he ses. "You'd be the same to me if you was dressed in rags."

He went upstairs without another word, and old Burge, who was coming down, came down five of 'em at once owing to Dixon speaking to 'im afore he knew who 'e was. The old man was still grumbling when Dixon came down agin, and said he believed he'd done it a-purpose.

"You run away from a good 'ome," he ses, "and the best wife in Wapping, and you come back and frighten people 'arf out o' their lives. I never see such a feller in all my born days."

"I was so glad to get 'ome agin I didn't think," ses Dixon. "I hope you're not 'urt."

He started telling them all about his 'ardships while they were at tea, but none of 'em seemed to care much about hearing 'em. Bob said that the sea was all right for men, and that other people were sure not to like it.

"And you brought it all on yourself," ses Charlie. "You've only got yourself to thank for it. I 'ad thought o' picking a bone with you over those letters you wrote."

"Let's 'ope 'e's come back more sensible than wot 'e was when 'e went away," ses old Burge, with 'is mouth full o' toast.

By the time he'd been back a couple o' days George Dixon could see that 'is going away 'adn't done any good at all. Nobody seemed to take any notice of 'im or wot he said, and at last, arter a word or two with Charlie about the rough way he spoke to some o' the customers, Charlie came in to Mrs. Dixon and said that he was at 'is old tricks of interfering, and he would not 'ave it.

"Well, he'd better keep out o' the bar altogether," ses Mrs. Dixon. "There's no need for 'im to go there; we managed all right while 'e was away."

"Do you mean I'm not to go into my own bar?" ses Dixon, stammering.

"Yes, I do," ses Mrs. Dixon. "You kept out of it for four years to please yourself, and now you can keep out of it to please me."

"I've put you out o' the bar before," ses Charlie, "and if you come messing about with me any more I'll do it agin. So now you know."

He walked back into the bar whistling, and George Dixon, arter sitting still for a long time thinking, got up and went into the bar, and he'd 'ardly got his foot inside afore Charlie caught 'old of 'im by the shoulder and shoved 'im back into the parlour agin.

"I told you wot it would be," ses Mrs. Dixon, looking up from 'er sewing. "You've only got your interfering ways to thank for it."

"This is a fine state of affairs in my own 'ouse," ses Dixon, 'ardly able to speak. "You've got no proper feeling for your husband, Julia, else you wouldn't allow it. Why, I was happier at sea than wot I am 'ere."

"Well, you'd better go back to it if you're so fond of it," ses 'is wife.

"I think I 'ad," ses Dixon. "If I can't be master in my own 'ouse I'm better at sea, hard as it is. You must choose between us, Julia—me or your relations. I won't sleep under the same roof as them for another night. Am I to go?"

"Please yourself," ses 'is wife. "I don't mind your staying 'ere so long as you behave yourself, but the others won't go; you can make your mind easy on that."

"I'll go and look for another ship, then," ses Dixon, taking up 'is cap. "I'm not wanted here. P'r'aps you wouldn't mind 'aving some clothes packed into a chest for me so as I can go away decent."

He looked round at 'is wife, as though 'e expected she'd ask 'im not to go, but she took no notice, and he opened the door softly and went out, while old Burge, who 'ad come into the room and 'eard what he was saying, trotted off upstairs to pack 'is chest for 'im.

In two hours 'e was back agin and more cheerful than he 'ad been since he 'ad come 'ome. Bob was in the bar and the others were just sitting down to tea, and a big chest, nicely corded, stood on the floor in the corner of the room.

"That's right," he ses, looking at it; "that's just wot I wanted."

"It's as full as it can be," ses old Burge. "I done it for you myself. 'Ave you got a ship?"

"I 'ave," ses Dixon. "A jolly good ship. No more hardships for me this time. I've got a berth as captain."

"Wot?" ses 'is wife. "Captain? You!"

"Yes," ses Dixon, smiling at her. "You can sail with me if you like."

"Thankee," ses Mrs. Dixon, "I'm quite comfortable where I am."

"Do you mean to say you've got a master's berth?" ses Charlie, staring at 'im.

"I do," ses Dixon; "master and owner."

Charlie coughed. "Wot's the name of the ship?" he asks, winking at the others.

"The BLUE LION," ses Dixon, in a voice that made 'em all start. "I'm shipping a new crew and I pay off the old one to-night. You first, my lad."

"Pay off," ses Charlie, leaning back in 'is chair and staring at 'im in a puzzled way. "Blue Lion?"

"Yes," ses Dixon, in the same loud voice. "When I came 'ome the other day I thought p'r'aps I'd let bygones be bygones, and I laid low for a bit to see whether any of you deserved it. I went to sea to get hardened—and I got hard. I've fought men that would eat you at a meal. I've 'ad more blows in a week than you've 'ad in a lifetime, you fat-faced land-lubber."

He walked to the door leading to the bar, where Bob was doing 'is best to serve customers and listen at the same time, and arter locking it put the key in 'is pocket. Then 'e put his 'and in 'is pocket and slapped some money down on the table in front o' Charlie.

"There's a month's pay instead o' notice," he ses. "Now git."

"George!" screams 'is wife. "'Ow dare you? 'Ave you gone crazy?"

"I'm surprised at you," ses old Burge, who'd been looking on with 'is mouth wide open, and pinching 'imself to see whether 'e wasn't dreaming.

"I don't go for your orders," ses Charlie, getting up. "Wot d'ye mean by locking that door?"

"Wot!" roars Dixon. "Hang it! I mustn't lock a door without asking my barman now. Pack up and be off, you swab, afore I start on you."

Charlie gave a growl and rushed at 'im, and the next moment 'e was down on the floor with the 'ardest bang in the face that he'd ever 'ad in 'is life. Mrs. Dixon screamed and ran into the kitchen, follered by old Burge, who went in to tell 'er not to be frightened. Charlie got up and went for Dixon agin; but he 'ad come back as 'ard as nails and 'ad a rushing style o' fighting that took Charlie's breath away. By the time Bob 'ad left the bar to take care of itself, and run round and got in the back way, Charlie had 'ad as much as 'e wanted and was lying on the sea-chest in the corner trying to get 'is breath.

"Yes? Wot d'ye want?" ses Dixon, with a growl, as Bob came in at the door.

He was such a 'orrible figure, with the blood on 'is face and 'is beard sticking out all ways, that Bob, instead of doing wot he 'ad come round for, stood in the doorway staring at 'im without a word.

"I'm paying off," ses Dixon. "'Ave you got any-thing to say agin it?"

"No," ses Bob, drawing back.

"You and Charlie'll go now," ses Dixon, taking out some money. "The old man can stay on for a month to give 'im time to look round. Don't look at me that way, else I'll knock your 'ead off."

He started counting out Bob's money just as old Burge and Mrs. Dixon, hearing all quiet, came in out of the kitchen.

"Don't you be alarmed on my account, my dear," he ses, turning to 'is wife; "it's child's play to wot I've been used to. I'll just see these two mistaken young fellers off the premises, and then we'll 'ave a cup o' tea while the old man minds the bar."

Mrs. Dixon tried to speak, but 'er temper was too much for 'er. She looked from her 'usband to Charlie and Bob and then back at 'im agin and caught 'er breath.

"That's right," ses Dixon, nodding his 'ead at her. "I'm master and owner of the Blue Lion and you're first mate. When I'm speaking you keep quiet; that's discipline."

I was in that bar about three months arterward, and I never saw such a change in any woman as there was in Mrs. Dixon. Of all the nice-mannered, soft-spoken landladies I've ever seen, she was the best, and on'y to 'ear the way she answered her 'usband when he spoke to 'er was a pleasure to every married man in the bar.

DOUBLE DEALING

Mr. Fred Carter stood on the spacious common, inhaling with all the joy of the holiday-making Londoner the salt smell of the sea below, and regarding with some interest the movements of a couple of men who had come to a stop a short distance away. As he looked they came on again, eying him closely as they approached—a strongly built, shambling man of fifty, and a younger man, evidently his son.

"Good-evening," said the former, as they came abreast of Mr. Carter.

"Good-evening," he replied.

"That's him," said both together.

They stood regarding him in a fashion unmistakably hostile. Mr. Carter, with an uneasy smile, awaited developments.

"What have you got to say for yourself?" demanded the elder man, at last. "Do you call yourself a man?"

"I don't call myself anything," said the puzzled Mr. Carter. "Perhaps you're mistaking me for somebody else."

"Didn't I tell you," said the younger man, turning to the other—"didn't I tell you he'd say that?"

"He can say what he likes," said the other, "but we've got him now. If he gets away from me he'll be cleverer than what he thinks he is."

"What are we to do with him now we've got him?" inquired his son.

The elder man clenched a huge fist and eyed Mr. Carter savagely. "If I was just considering myself," he said, "I should hammer him till I was tired and then chuck him into the sea."

His son nodded. "That wouldn't do Nancy much good, though," he remarked.

"I want to do everything for the best," said the other, "and I s'pose the right and proper thing to do is to take him by the scruff of his neck and run him along to Nancy."

"You try it," said Mr. Carter, hotly. "Who is Nancy?"

The other growled, and was about to aim a blow at him when his son threw himself upon him and besought him to be calm.

"Just one," said his father, struggling, "only one. It would do me good; and perhaps he'd come along the quieter for it."

"Look here!" said Mr. Carter. "You're mistaking me for somebody else, that's what you are doing. What am I supposed to have done?"

"You're supposed to have come courting my daughter, Mr. Somebody Else," said the other, re-leasing himself and thrusting his face into Mr. Carter's, "and, after getting her promise to marry you, nipping off to London to arrange for the wedding. She's been mourning over you for four years now, having an idea that you had been made away with."

"Being true to your memory, you skunk," said the son.

"And won't look at decent chaps that want to marry her," added the other.

"It's all a mistake," said Mr. Carter. "I came down here this morning for the first time in my life."

"Bring him along," said the son, impatiently. "It's a waste of time talking to him."

Mr. Carter took a step back and parleyed. "I'll come along with you of my own free will," he said, hastily, "just to show you that you are wrong; but I won't be forced."

He turned and walked back with them towards the town, pausing occasionally to admire the view. Once he paused so long that an ominous growl arose from the elder of his captors.

"I was just thinking," said Mr. Carter, eying him in consternation; "suppose that she makes the same mistake that you have made? Oh, Lord!"

"Keeps it up pretty well, don't he, Jim?" said the father.

The other grunted and, drawing nearer to Mr. Carter as they entered the town, stepped along in silence. Questions which Mr. Carter asked with the laudable desire of showing his ignorance concerning the neighborhood elicited no reply. His discomfiture was increased by the behavior of an elderly boatman, who, after looking at him hard, took his pipe from his mouth and bade him "Good-evening." Father and son exchanged significant glances.

They turned at last into a small street, and the elder man, opening the door of a neat cottage, laid his hand on the prisoner's shoulder and motioned him in. Mr. Carter obeyed, and, entering a spotless living-room, removed his hat and with affected composure seated himself in an easy-chair.

"I'll go up and tell Nan," said Jim. "Don't let him run away."

He sprang up the stairs, which led from a corner of the room, and the next moment the voice of a young lady, laboring under intense excitement, fell on the ears of Mr. Carter. With a fine attempt at unconcern he rose and inspected an aged engraving of "The Sailor's Return."

"She'll be down in a minute," said Jim, returning

"P'r'aps it's as well that I didn't set about him, after all," said his father. "If I had done what I should like to do, his own mother wouldn't have known him."

Mr. Carter sniffed defiantly and, with a bored air, resumed his seat. Ten minutes passed—fifteen; at the end of half an hour the elder man's impatience found vent in a tirade against the entire sex.

"She's dressing up; that's what it is," explained Jim. "For him!"

A door opened above and a step sounded on the stairs. Mr. Carter looked up uneasily, and, after the first sensation of astonishment had passed, wondered vaguely what his double had run away for. The girl, her lips parted and her eyes bright, came swiftly down into the room.

"Where is he?" she said, quickly.

"Eh?" said her father, in surprise. "Why, there! Can't you see?"

The light died out of the girl's face and she looked round in dismay. The watchful Mr. Carter thought that he also detected in her glance a spice of that temper which had made her relatives so objectionable.

"That!" she said, loudly. "That! That's not my Bert!"

"That's what I told 'em," said Mr. Carter, deferentially, "over and over again."

"What!" said her father, loudly. "Look again."

"If I looked all night it wouldn't make any difference," said the disappointed Miss Evans. "The idea of making such a mistake!"

"We're all liable to mistakes," said Mr. Carter, magnanimously, "even the best of us."

"You take a good look at him," urged her brother, "and don't forget that it's four years since you saw him. Isn't that Bert's nose?"

"No," said the girl, glancing at the feature in question, "not a bit like it. Bert had a beautiful nose."

"Look at his eyes," said Jim.

Miss Evans looked, and meeting Mr. Carter's steady gaze tossed her head scornfully and endeavored to stare him down. Realizing too late the magnitude of the task, but unwilling to accept defeat, she stood confronting him with indignant eyes.

"Well?" said Mr. Evans, misunderstanding.

"Not a bit like," said his daughter, turning thank-fully. "And if you don't like Bert, you needn't insult him."

She sat down with her back towards Mr. Carter and looked out at the window.

"Well, I could ha' sworn it was Bert Simmons," said the discomfited Mr. Evans.

"Me, too," said his son. "I'd ha' sworn to him anywhere. It's the most extraordinary likeness I've ever seen."

He caught his father's eye, and with a jerk of his thumb telegraphed for instructions as to the disposal of Mr. Carter.

"He can go," said Mr. Evans, with an attempt at dignity; "he can go this time, and I hope that this'll be a lesson to him not to go about looking like other people. If he does, next time, p'r'aps, he won't escape so easy."

"You're quite right," said Mr. Carter, blandly. "I'll get a new face first thing to-morrow morning. I ought to have done it before."

He crossed to the door and, nodding to the fermenting Mr. Evans, bowed to the profile of Miss Evans and walked slowly out. Envy of Mr. Simmons was mingled with amazement at his deplorable lack of taste and common sense. He would willingly have changed places with him. There was evidently a strong likeness, and—

Busy with his thoughts he came to a standstill in the centre of the footpath, and then, with a sudden air of determination, walked slowly back to the house.

"Yes?" said Mr. Evans, as the door opened and the face of Mr. Carter was thrust in. "What have you come back for?"

The other stepped into the room and closed the door softly behind him. "I have come back," he said, slowly—"I have come back because I feel ashamed of myself."

"Ashamed of yourself?" repeated Mr. Evans, rising and confronting him.

Mr. Carter hung his head and gazed nervously in the direction of the girl. "I can't keep up this deception," he said, in a low but distinct voice. "I am Bert Simmons. At least, that is the name I told you four years ago."

"I knew I hadn't made a mistake," roared Mr. Evans to his son. "I knew him well enough. Shut the door, Jim. Don't let him go."

"I don't want to go," said Mr. Carter, with a glance in the direction of Nancy. "I have come back to make amends."

"Fancy Nancy not knowing him!" said Jim, gazing at the astonished Miss Evans.

"She was afraid of getting me into trouble," said Mr. Carter, "and I just gave her a wink not to recognize me; but she knew me well enough, bless her."

"How dare you!" said the girl, starting up. "Why, I've never seen you before in my life."

"All right, Nan," said the brazen Mr. Carter; "but it's no good keeping it up now. I've come back to act fair and square."

Miss Evans struggled for breath.

"There he is, my girl," said her father, patting her on the back. "He's not much to look at, and he treated you very shabby, but if you want him I suppose you must have him."

"Want him?" repeated the incensed Miss Evans. "Want him? I tell you it's not Bert. How dare he come here and call me Nan?"

"You used not to mind it," said Mr. Carter, plaintively.

"I tell you," said Miss Evans, turning to her father and brother, "it's not Bert. Do you think I don't know?"

"Well, he ought to know who he is," said her father, reasonably.

"Of course I ought," said Mr. Carter, smiling at her. "Besides, what reason should I have for saying I am Bert if I am not?"

"That's a fair question," said Jim, as the girl bit her lip. "Why should he?"

"Ask him," said the girl, tartly.

"Look here, my girl," said Mr. Evans, in ominous accents. "For four years you've been grieving over Bert, and me and Jim have been hunting high and low for him. We've got him at last, and now you've got to have him."

"If he don't run away again," said Jim. "I wouldn't trust him farther than I could see him."

Mr. Evans sat and glowered at his prospective son-in-law as the difficulties of the situation developed themselves. Even Mr. Carter's reminders that he had come back and surrendered of his own free will failed to move him, and he was hesitating between tying him up and locking him in the attic and hiring a man to watch him, when Mr. Carter himself suggested a way out of the difficulty.

"I'll lodge with you," he said, "and I'll give you all my money and things to take care of. I can't run away without money."

He turned out his pockets on the table. Seven pounds eighteen shillings and fourpence with his return ticket made one heap; his watch and chain, penknife, and a few other accessories another. A suggestion of Jim's that he should add his boots was vetoed by the elder man as unnecessary.

"There you are," said Mr. Evans, sweeping the things into his own pockets; "and the day you are married I hand them back to you."

His temper improved as the evening wore on. By the time supper was finished and his pipe alight he became almost jocular, and the coldness of Miss Evans was the only drawback to an otherwise enjoyable evening.

"Just showing off a little temper," said her father, after she had withdrawn; "and wants to show she ain't going to forgive you too easy. Not but what you behaved badly; however, let bygones be bygones, that's my idea."

The behavior of Miss Evans was so much better next day that it really seemed as though her father's diagnosis was correct. At dinner, when the men came home from work, she piled Mr. Carter's plate up so generously that her father and brother had ample time at their disposal to watch him eat. And when he put his hand over his glass she poured half a pint of good beer, that other men would have been thankful for, up his sleeve.

She was out all the afternoon, but at tea time she sat next to Mr. Carter, and joined brightly in the conversation concerning her marriage. She addressed him as Bert, and when he furtively pressed her hand beneath the table-cloth she made no attempt to withdraw it.

"I can't think how it was you didn't know him at first," said her father. "You're usually wide-awake enough."

"Silly of me," said Nancy; "but I am silly sometimes."

Mr. Carter pressed her hand again, and gazing tenderly into her eyes received a glance in return which set him thinking. It was too cold and calculating for real affection; in fact, after another glance, he began to doubt if it indicated affection at all.

"It's like old times, Bert," said Miss Evans, with an odd smile. "Do you remember what you said that afternoon when I put the hot spoon on your neck?"

"Yes," was the reply.

"What was it?" inquired the girl.

"I won't repeat it," said Mr. Carter, firmly.

He was reminded of other episodes during the meal, but, by the exercise of tact and the plea of a bad memory, did fairly well. He felt that he had done very well indeed when, having cleared the tea-things away, Nancy came and sat beside him with her hand in his. Her brother grunted, but Mr. Evans, in whom a vein of sentiment still lingered, watched them with much satisfaction.

Mr. Carter had got possession of both hands and was murmuring fulsome flatteries when the sound of somebody pausing at the open door caused them to be hastily withdrawn.

"Evening, Mr. Evans," said a young man, putting his head in. "Why, halloa! Bert! Well, of all the—"

"Halloa!" said Mr. Carter, with attempted enthusiasm, as he rose from his chair.

"I thought you was lost," said the other, stepping in and gripping his hand. "I never thought I was going to set eyes on you again. Well, this is a surprise. You ain't forgot Joe Wilson, have you?"

"Course I haven't, Joe," said Mr. Carter. "I'd have known you anywhere."

He shook hands effusively, and Mr. Wilson, after a little pretended hesitation, accepted a chair and began to talk about old times.

"I lay you ain't forgot one thing, Bert," he said at last.

"What's that?" inquired the other.

"That arf-quid I lent you," said Mr. Wilson.

Mr. Carter, after the first shock of surprise, pretended to think, Mr. Wilson supplying him with details as to time and place, which he was in no position to dispute. He turned to Mr. Evans, who was still acting as his banker, and, after a little hesitation, requested him to pay the money. Conversation seemed to fail somewhat after that, and Mr. Wilson, during an awkward pause, went off whistling.

"Same old Joe," said Mr. Carter, lightly, after he had gone. "He hasn't altered a bit."

Miss Evans glanced at him, but said nothing. She was looking instead towards a gentleman of middle age who was peeping round the door indulging in a waggish game of peep-bo with the unconscious Mr. Carter. Finding that he had at last attracted his attention, the gentleman came inside and, breathing somewhat heavily after his exertions, stood before him with outstretched hand.

"How goes it?" said Mr. Carter, forcing a smile and shaking hands.

"He's grown better-looking than ever," said the gentleman, subsiding into a chair.

"So have you," said Mr. Carter. "I should hardly have known you."

"Well, I' m glad to see you again," said the other in a more subdued fashion. "We're all glad to see you back, and I 'ope that when the wedding cake is sent out there'll be a bit for old Ben Prout."

"You'll be the first, Ben," said Mr. Carter, quickly.

Mr. Prout got up and shook hands with him again. "It only shows what mistakes a man can make," he said, resuming his seat. "It only shows how easy it is to misjudge one's fellow-creeturs. When you went away sudden four years ago, I says to myself, 'Ben Prout,' I says, 'make up your mind to it, that two quid has gorn.'"

The smile vanished from Mr. Carter's face, and a sudden chill descended upon the company.

"Two quid?" he said, stiffly. "What two quid?"

"The two quid I lent you," said Mr. Prout, in a pained voice.

"When?" said Mr. Carter, struggling.

"When you and I met him that evening on the pier," said Miss Evans, in a matter-of-fact voice.

Mr. Carter started, and gazed at her uneasily. The smile on her lip and the triumphant gleam in her eye were a revelation to him. He turned to Mr. Evans and in as calm a voice as he could assume, requested him to discharge the debt. Mr. Prout, his fingers twitching, stood waiting "Well, it's your money," said Mr. Evans, grudgingly extracting a purse from his trouser-pocket; "and I suppose you ought to pay your debts; still—"

He put down two pounds on the table and broke off in sudden amazement as Mr. Prout, snatching up the money, bolted headlong from the room. His surprise was shared by his son, but the other two made no sign. Mr. Carter was now prepared for the worst, and his voice was quite calm as he gave instructions for the payment of the other three gentlemen who presented claims during the evening endorsed by Miss Evans. As the last departed Mr. Evans, whose temper had been gradually getting beyond his control, crossed over and handed him his watch and chain, a few coppers, and the return half of his railway ticket.

"I think we can do without you, after all," he said, breathing thickly. "I've no doubt you owe money all over England. You're a cadger, that's what you are."

He pointed to the door, and Mr. Carter, after twice opening his lips to speak and failing, blundered towards it. Miss Evans watched him curiously.

"Cheats never prosper," she said, with gentle severity.

"Good-by," said Mr. Carter, pausing at the door.

"It's your own fault," continued Miss Evans, who was suffering from a slight touch of conscience. "If you hadn't come here pretending to be Bert Simmons and calling me 'Nan' as if you had known me all my life, I wouldn't have done it."

"It doesn't matter," said Mr. Carter. "I wish I was Bert Simmons, that's all. Good-by."

"Wish you was!" said Mr. Evans, who had been listening in open-mouthed astonishment. "Look here! Man to man—are you Bert Simmons or are you not?"

"No," said Mr. Carter.

"Of course not," said Nancy.

"And you didn't owe that money?"

"Nobody owed it," said Nancy. "It was done just to punish him."

Mr. Evans, with a strange cry, blundered towards the door. "I'll have that money out of 'em," he roared, "if I have to hold 'em up and shake it out of their trouser-pockets. You stay here."

He hurried up the road, and Jim, with the set face of a man going into action against heavy odds, followed him.

"Your father told me to stay," said Mr. Carter, coming farther into the room.

Nancy looked up at him through her eyelashes. "You need not unless you want to," she said, very softly.

THE DREAMER

Dreams and warnings are things I don't believe in, said the night watchman. The only dream I ever 'ad that come anything like true was once when I dreamt I came in for a fortune, and next morning I found half a crown in the street, which I sold to a man for fourpence. And once, two days arter my missis 'ad dreamt she 'ad spilt a cup of tea down the front of 'er Sunday dress, she spoilt a pot o' paint of mine by sitting in it.

The only other dream I know of that come true happened to the cook of a bark I was aboard of once, called the Southern Belle. He was a silly, pasty-faced sort o' chap, always giving hisself airs about eddication to sailormen who didn't believe in it, and one night, when we was homeward-bound from Sydney, he suddenly sat up in 'is bunk and laughed so loud that he woke us all up.

"Wot's wrong, cookie?" ses one o' the chaps.

"I was dreaming," ses the cook, "such a funny dream. I dreamt old Bill Foster fell out o' the foretop and broke 'is leg."

"Well, wot is there to laugh at in that?" ses old Bill, very sharp.

"It was funny in my dream," ses the cook. "You looked so comic with your leg doubled up under you, you can't think. It would ha' made a cat laugh."

Bill Foster said he'd make 'im laugh the other side of his face if he wasn't careful, and then we went off to sleep agin and forgot all about it.

If you'll believe me, on'y three days arterwards pore Bill did fall out o' the foretop and break his leg. He was surprised, but I never see a man so surprised as the cook was. His eyes was nearly starting out of 'is head, but by the time the other chaps 'ad picked Bill up and asked 'im whether he was hurt, cook 'ad pulled 'imself together agin and was giving himself such airs it was perfectly sickening.

"My dreams always come true," he ses. "It's a kind o' second sight with me. It's a gift, and, being tender-'arted, it worries me terrible sometimes."

He was going on like that, taking credit for a pure accident, when the second officer came up and told 'em to carry Bill below. He was in agony, of course, but he kept 'is presence of mind, and as they passed the cook he gave 'im such a clip on the side of the 'ead as nearly broke it.

"That's for dreaming about me," he ses.

The skipper and the fust officer and most of the hands set 'is leg between them, and arter the skipper 'ad made him wot he called comfortable, but wot Bill called something that I won't soil my ears by repeating, the officers went off and the cook came and sat down by the side o' Bill and talked about his gift.

"I don't talk about it as a rule," he ses, "'cos it frightens people."

"It's a wonderful gift, cookie," ses Charlie Epps.

All of 'em thought the same, not knowing wot a fust-class liar the cook was, and he sat there and lied to 'em till he couldn't 'ardly speak, he was so 'oarse.

"My grandmother was a gypsy," he ses, "and it's in the family. Things that are going to 'appen to people I know come to me in dreams, same as pore Bill's did. It's curious to me sometimes when I look round at you chaps, seeing you going about 'appy and comfortable, and knowing all the time 'orrible things that is going to 'appen to you. Sometimes it gives me the fair shivers."

"Horrible things to us, slushy?" ses Charlie, staring.

"Yes," ses the cook, nodding. "I never was on a ship afore with such a lot of unfortunit men aboard. Never. There's two pore fellers wot'll be dead corpses inside o' six months, sitting 'ere laughing and talking as if they was going to live to ninety. Thank your stars you don't 'ave such dreams."

"Who—who are the two, cookie?" ses Charlie, arter a bit.

"Never mind, Charlie," ses the cook, in a sad voice; "it would do no good if I was to tell you. Nothing can alter it."

"Give us a hint," ses Charlie.

"Well, I'll tell you this much," ses the cook, arter sitting with his 'ead in his 'ands, thinking; "one of 'em is nearly the ugliest man in the fo'c's'le and the other ain't."

O' course, that didn't 'elp 'em much, but it caused a lot of argufying, and the ugliest man aboard, instead o' being grateful, behaved more like a wild beast than a Christian when it was pointed out to him that he was safe.

Arter that dream about Bill, there was no keeping the cook in his place. He 'ad dreams pretty near every night, and talked little bits of 'em in his sleep. Little bits that you couldn't make head nor tail of, and when we asked 'im next morning he'd always shake his 'ead and say, "Never mind." Sometimes he'd mention a chap's name in 'is sleep and make 'im nervous for days.

It was an unlucky v'y'ge that, for some of 'em. About a week arter pore Bill's accident Ted Jones started playing catch-ball with another chap and a empty beer-bottle, and about the fifth chuck Ted caught it with his face. We thought 'e was killed at fust—he made such a noise; but they got 'im down below, and, arter they 'ad picked out as much broken glass as Ted would let 'em, the second officer did 'im up in sticking-plaster and told 'im to keep quiet for an hour or two.

Ted was very proud of 'is looks, and the way he went on was alarming. Fust of all he found fault with the chap 'e was playing with, and then he turned on the cook.

"It's a pity you didn't see that in a dream," he ses, tryin' to sneer, on'y the sticking-plaster was too strong for 'im.

"But I did see it," ses the cook, drawin' 'imself up.

"Wot?" ses Ted, starting.

"I dreamt it night afore last, just exactly as it 'appened," ses the cook, in a offhand way.

"Why didn't you tell me, then?" ses Ted choking.

"It 'ud ha' been no good," ses the cook, smiling and shaking his 'ead. "Wot I see must 'appen. I on'y see the future, and that must be."

"But you stood there watching me chucking the bottle about," ses Ted, getting out of 'is bunk. "Why didn't you stop me?"

"You don't understand," ses the cook. "If you'd 'ad more eddication—"

He didn't 'ave time to say any more afore Ted was on him, and cookie, being no fighter, 'ad to cook with one eye for the next two or three days. He kept quiet about 'is dreams for some time arter that, but it was no good, because George Hall, wot was a firm believer, gave 'im a licking for not warning 'im of a sprained ankle he got skylarking, and Bob Law took it out of 'im for not telling 'im that he was going to lose 'is suit of shore-going togs at cards.

The only chap that seemed to show any good feeling for the cook was a young feller named Joseph Meek, a steady young chap wot was goin' to be married to old Bill Foster's niece as soon as we got 'ome. Nobody else knew it, but he told the cook all about it on the quiet. He said she was too good for 'im, but, do all he could, he couldn't get her to see it.

"My feelings 'ave changed," he ses.

"P'r'aps they'll change agin," ses the cook, trying to comfort 'im.

Joseph shook his 'ead. "No, I've made up my mind," he ses, very slow. "I'm young yet, and, besides, I can't afford it; but 'ow to get out of it I don't know. Couldn't you 'ave a dream agin it for me?"

"Wot d'ye mean?" ses the cook, firing up. "Do you think I make my dreams up?"

"No, no; cert'inly not," ses Joseph, patting 'im on the shoulder; "but couldn't you do it just for once? 'Ave a dream that me and Emily are killed a few days arter the wedding. Don't say in wot way, 'cos she might think we could avoid it; just dream we are killed. Bill's always been a superstitious man, and since you dreamt about his leg he'd believe anything; and he's that fond of Emily I believe he'd 'ave the wedding put off, at any rate—if I put him up to it."

It took 'im three days and a silver watch-chain to persuade the cook, but he did at last; and one arternoon, when old Bill, who was getting on fust-class, was resting 'is leg in 'is bunk, the cook went below and turned in for a quiet sleep.

For ten minutes he was as peaceful as a lamb, and old Bill, who 'ad been laying in 'is bunk with an eye open watching 'im, was just dropping off 'imself, when the cook began to talk in 'is sleep, and the very fust words made Bill sit up as though something 'ad bit 'im.

"There they go," ses the cook, "Emily Foster and Joseph Meek—and there's old Bill, good old Bill, going to give the bride away. How 'appy they all look, especially Joseph!"

Old Bill put his 'and to his ear and leaned out of his bunk.

"There they go," ses the cook agin; "but wot is that 'orrible black thing with claws that's 'anging over Bill?"

Pore Bill nearly fell out of 'is bunk, but he saved 'imself at the last moment and lay there as pale as death, listening.

"It must be meant for Bill," ses the cook. "Well, pore Bill; he won't know of it, that's one thing. Let's 'ope it'll be sudden."

He lay quiet for some time and then he began again.

"No," he ses, "it isn't Bill; it's Joseph and Emily, stark and stiff, and they've on'y been married a week. 'Ow awful they look! Pore things. Oh! oh! o-oh!"

He woke up with a shiver and began to groan and then 'e sat up in his bunk and saw old Bill leaning out and staring at 'im.

"You've been dreaming, cook," ses Bill, in a trembling voice.

"'Ave I?" ses the cook. "How do you know?"

"About me and my niece," ses Bill; "you was talking in your sleep."

"You oughtn't to 'ave listened," ses the cook, getting out of 'is bunk and going over to 'im. "I 'ope you didn't 'ear all I dreamt. 'Ow much did you hear?"

Bill told 'im, and the cook sat there, shaking his 'ead. "Thank goodness, you didn't 'ear the worst of it," he ses.

"Worst!" ses Bill. "Wot, was there any more of it?"

"Lot's more," ses the cook. "But promise me you won't tell Joseph, Bill. Let 'im be happy while he can; it would on'y make 'im miserable, and it wouldn't do any good."

"I don't know so much about that," ses Bill, thinking about the arguments some of them had 'ad with Ted about the bottle. "Was it arter they was married, cookie, that it 'appened? Are you sure?"

"Certain sure. It was a week arter," ses the cook.

"Very well, then," ses Bill, slapping 'is bad leg by mistake; "if they didn't marry, it couldn't 'appen, could it?"

"Don't talk foolish," ses the cook; "they must marry. I saw it in my dream."

"Well, we'll see," ses Bill. "I'm going to 'ave a quiet talk with Joseph about it, and see wot he ses. I ain't a-going to 'ave my pore gal murdered just to please you and make your dreams come true."

He 'ad a quiet talk with Joseph, but Joseph wouldn't 'ear of it at fust. He said it was all the cook's nonsense, though 'e owned up that it was funny that the cook should know about the wedding and Emily's name, and at last he said that they would put it afore Emily and let her decide.

That was about the last dream the cook had that v'y'ge, although he told old Bill one day that he had 'ad the same dream about Joseph and Emily agin, so that he was quite certain they 'ad got to be married and killed. He wouldn't tell Bill 'ow they was to be killed, because 'e said it would make 'im an old man afore his time; but, of course, he 'ad to say that if they wasn't married the other part couldn't come true. He said that as he 'ad never told 'is dreams before—except in the case of Bill's leg—he couldn't say for certain that they couldn't be prevented by taking care, but p'r'aps, they could; and Bill pointed out to 'im wot a useful man he would be if he could dream and warn people in time.

By the time we got into the London river old Bill's leg was getting on fust-rate, and he got along splendid on a pair of crutches the carpenter 'ad made for him. Him and Joseph and the cook had 'ad a good many talks about the dream, and the old man 'ad invited the cook to come along 'ome with 'em, to be referred to when he told the tale.

"I shall take my opportunity," he ses, "and break it to 'er gentle like. When I speak to you, you chip in, and not afore. D'ye understand?"

We went into the East India Docks that v'y'ge, and got there early on a lovely summer's evening. Everybody was 'arf crazy at the idea o' going ashore agin, and working as cheerful and as willing as if they liked it. There was a few people standing on the pier-head as we went in, and among 'em several very nice-looking young wimmen.

"My eye, Joseph," ses the cook, who 'ad been staring hard at one of 'em, "there's a fine gal—lively, too. Look 'ere!"

He kissed 'is dirty paw—which is more than I should 'ave liked to 'ave done it if it 'ad been mine—and waved it, and the gal turned round and shook her 'ead at 'im.

"Here, that'll do," ses Joseph, very cross. "That's my gal; that's my Emily."

"Eh?" says the cook. "Well, 'ow was I to know? Besides, you're a-giving of her up."

Joseph didn't answer 'im. He was staring at Emily, and the more he stared the better-looking she seemed to grow. She really was an uncommon nice-looking gal, and more than the cook was struck with her.

"Who's that chap standing alongside of her?" ses the cook.

"It's one o' Bill's sister's lodgers," ses Joseph, who was looking very bad-tempered. "I should like to know wot right he 'as to come 'ere to welcome me 'ome. I don't want 'im."

"P'r'aps he's fond of 'er," ses the cook. "I could be, very easy."

"I'll chuck 'im in the dock if he ain't careful," ses Joseph, turning red in the face.

He waved his 'and to Emily, who didn't 'appen to be looking at the moment, but the lodger waved back in a careless sort of way and then spoke to Emily, and they both waved to old Bill who was standing on his crutches further aft.

By the time the ship was berthed and everything snug it was quite dark, and old Bill didn't know whether to take the cook 'ome with 'im and break the news that night, or wait a bit. He made up his mind at last to get it over and done with, and arter waiting till the cook 'ad cleaned 'imself they got a cab and drove off.

Bert Simmons, the lodger, 'ad to ride on the box, and Bill took up so much room with 'is bad leg that Emily found it more comfortable to sit on Joseph's knee; and by the time they got to the 'ouse he began to see wot a silly mistake he was making.

"Keep that dream o' yours to yourself till I make up my mind," he ses to the cook, while Bill and the cabman were calling each other names.

"Bill's going to speak fust," whispers the cook.

The lodger and Emily 'ad gone inside, and Joseph stood there, fidgeting, while the cabman asked Bill, as a friend, why he 'adn't paid twopence more for his face, and Bill was wasting his time trying to think of something to say to 'urt the cabman's feelings. Then he took Bill by the arm as the cab drove off and told 'im not to say nothing about the dream, because he was going to risk it.

"Stuff and nonsense," ses Bill. "I'm going to tell Emily. It's my dooty. Wot's the good o' being married if you're going to be killed?"

He stumped in on his crutches afore Joseph could say any more, and, arter letting his sister kiss 'im, went into the front room and sat down. There was cold beef and pickles on the table and two jugs o' beer, and arter just telling his sister 'ow he fell and broke 'is leg, they all sat down to supper.

Bert Simmons sat on one side of Emily and Joseph the other, and the cook couldn't 'elp feeling sorry for 'er, seeing as he did that sometimes she was 'aving both hands squeezed at once under the table and could 'ardly get a bite in edgeways.

Old Bill lit his pipe arter supper, and then, taking another glass o' beer, he told 'em about the cook dreaming of his accident three days afore it happened. They couldn't 'ardly believe it at fust, but when he went on to tell 'em the other things the cook 'ad dreamt, and that everything 'ad 'appened just as he dreamt it, they all edged away from the cook and sat staring at him with their mouths open.

"And that ain't the worst of it," ses Bill.

"That's enough for one night, Bill," ses Joseph, who was staring at Bert Simmons as though he could eat him. "Besides, I believe it was on'y chance. When cook told you 'is dream it made you nervous, and that's why you fell."

"Nervous be blowed!" ses Bill; and then he told 'em about the dream he 'ad heard while he was laying in 'is bunk.

Bill's sister gave a scream when he 'ad finished, and Emily, wot was sitting next to Joseph, got up with a shiver and went and sat next to Bert Simmons and squeezed his coat-sleeve.

"It's all nonsense!" ses Joseph, starting up. "And if it wasn't, true love would run the risk. I ain't afraid!"

"It's too much to ask a gal," ses Bert Simmons, shaking his 'ead.

"I couldn't dream of it," ses Emily. "Wot's the use of being married for a week? Look at uncle's leg— that's enough for me!"

They all talked at once then, and Joseph tried all he could to persuade Emily to prove to the cook that 'is dreams didn't always come true; but it was no good. Emily said she wouldn't marry 'im if he 'ad a million a year, and her aunt and uncle backed her up in it—to say nothing of Bert Simmons.

"I'll go up and get your presents, Joseph," she ses; and she ran upstairs afore anybody could stop her.

Joseph sat there as if he was dazed, while everybody gave 'im good advice, and said 'ow thankful he ought to be that the cook 'ad saved him by 'is dreaming. And by and by Emily came downstairs agin with the presents he 'ad given 'er and put them on the table in front of 'im.

"There's everything there but that little silver brooch you gave me, Joseph," she ses, "and I lost that the other evening when I was out with—with—for a walk."

Joseph tried to speak, but couldn't.

"It was six-and-six, 'cos I was with you when you bought it," ses Emily; "and as I've lost it, it's on'y fair I should pay for it."

She put down 'arf a sovereign with the presents, and Joseph sat staring at it as if he 'ad never seen one afore.

"And you needn't mind about the change, Joseph," ses Emily; "that'll 'elp to make up for your disappointment."

Old Bill tried to turn things off with a bit of a laugh. "Why, you're made o' money, Emily," he ses.

"Ah! I haven't told you yet," ses Emily, smiling at him; "that's a little surprise I was keeping for you. Aunt Emma—pore Aunt Emma, I should say—died while you was away and left me all 'er furniture and two hundred pounds."

Joseph made a choking noise in his throat and then 'e got up, leaving the presents and the 'arf-sovereign on the table, and stood by the door, staring at them.

"Good-night all," he ses. Then he went to the front door and opened it, and arter standing there a moment came back as though he 'ad forgotten something.

"Are you coming along now?" he ses to the cook.

"Not just yet," ses the cook, very quick.

"I'll wait outside for you, then," ses Joseph, grinding his teeth. "Don't be long."

DUAL CONTROL

"Never say 'die,' Bert," said Mr. Culpepper, kindly; "I like you, and so do most other people who know what's good for 'em; and if Florrie don't like you she can keep single till she does."

Mr. Albert Sharp thanked him.

"Come in more oftener," said Mr. Culpepper. "If she don't know a steady young man when she sees him, it's her mistake."

"Nobody could be steadier than what I am," sighed Mr. Sharp.

Mr. Culpepper nodded. "The worst of it is, girls don't like steady young men," he said, rumpling his thin grey hair; "that's the silly part of it."

"But you was always steady, and Mrs. Culpepper married you," said the young man.

Mr. Culpepper nodded again. "She thought I was, and that came to the same thing," he said, composedly. "And it ain't for me to say, but she had an idea that I was very good-looking in them days. I had chestnutty hair. She burnt a piece of it only the other day she'd kept for thirty years."

"Burnt it? What for?" inquired Mr. Sharp.

"Words," said the other, lowering his voice. "When I want one thing nowadays she generally wants another; and the things she wants ain't the things I want."

Mr. Sharp shook his head and sighed again.

"You ain't talkative enough for Florrie, you know," said Mr. Culpepper, regarding him.

"I can talk all right as a rule," retorted Mr. Sharp. "You ought to hear me at the debating society; but you can't talk to a girl who doesn't talk back."

"You're far too humble," continued the other. "You should cheek her a bit now and then. Let 'er see you've got some spirit. Chaff 'er."

"That's no good," said the young man, restlessly. "I've tried it. Only the other day I called her 'a saucy little kipper,' and the way she went on, anybody would have thought I'd insulted her. Can't see a joke, I s'pose. Where is she now?"

"Upstairs," was the reply.

"That's because I'm here," said Mr. Sharp. "If it had been Jack Butler she'd have been down fast enough."

"It couldn't be him," said Mr. Culpepper, "because I won't have 'im in the house. I've told him so; I've told her so, and I've told 'er aunt so. And if she marries without my leave afore she's thirty she loses the seven hundred pounds 'er father left her. You've got plenty of time—ten years."

Mr. Sharp, sitting with his hands between his knees, gazed despondently at the floor. "There's a lot o' girls would jump at me," he remarked. "I've only got to hold up my little finger and they'd jump."

"That's because they've got sense," said Mr. Culpepper. "They've got the sense to prefer steadiness and humdrumness to good looks and dash. A young fellow like you earning thirty-two-and-six a week can do without good looks, and if I've told Florrie so once I have told her fifty times."

"Looks are a matter of taste," said Mr. Sharp, morosely. "Some of them girls I was speaking about just now—"

"Yes, yes," said Mr. Culpepper, hastily. "Now, look here; you go on a different tack. Take a glass of ale like a man or a couple o' glasses; smoke a cigarette or a pipe. Be like other young men. Cut a dash, and don't be a namby-pamby. After you're married you can be as miserable as you like."

Mr. Sharp, after a somewhat lengthy interval, thanked him.

"It's my birthday next Wednesday," continued Mr. Culpepper, regarding him benevolently; "come round about seven, and I'll ask you to stay to supper. That'll give you a chance. Anybody's allowed to step a bit over the mark on birthdays, and you might take a glass or two and make a speech, and be so happy and bright that they'd 'ardly know you. If you want an excuse for calling, you could bring me a box of cigars for my birthday."

"Or come in to wish you 'Many Happy Returns of the Day,'" said the thrifty Mr. Sharp.

"And don't forget to get above yourself," said Mr. Culpepper, regarding him sternly; "in a gentlemanly way, of course. Have as many glasses as you like—there's no stint about me."

"If it ever comes off," said Mr. Sharp, rising—"if I get her through you, you shan't have reason to repent it. I'll look after that."

Mr. Culpepper, whose feelings were a trifle ruffled, said that he would "look after it too." He had a faint idea that, even from his own point of view, he might have made a better selection for his niece's hand.

Mr. Sharp smoked his first cigarette the following morning, and, encouraged by the entire absence of any after-effects, purchased a pipe, which was taken up by a policeman the same evening for obstructing the public footpath in company with a metal tobacco-box three parts full.

In the matter of ale he found less difficulty. Certainly the taste was unpleasant, but, treated as medicine and gulped down quickly, it was endurable. After a day or two he even began to be critical, and on Monday evening went so far as to complain of its flatness to the wide-eyed landlord of the "Royal George."

"Too much cellar-work," he said, as he finished his glass and made for the door.

"Too much! 'Ere, come 'ere," said the landlord, thickly. "I want to speak to you."

The expert shook his head, and, passing out into, the street, changed colour as he saw Miss Garland approaching. In a blundering fashion he clutched at his hat and stammered out a "Good evening."

Miss Garland returned the greeting and, instead of passing on, stopped and, with a friendly smile, held out her hand. Mr. Sharp shook it convulsively.

"You are just the man I want to see," she exclaimed. "Aunt and I have been talking about you all the afternoon."

Mr. Sharp said "Really!"

"But I don't want uncle to see us," pursued Miss Garland, in the low tones of confidence. "Which way shall we go?"

Mr. Sharp's brain reeled. All ways were alike to him in such company. He walked beside her like a man in a dream.

"We want to give him a lesson," said the girl, presently. "A lesson that he will remember."

"Him?" said the young man.

"Uncle," explained the girl. "It's a shocking thing, a wicked thing, to try and upset a steady young man like you. Aunt is quite put out about it, and I feel the same as she does."

"But," gasped the astonished Mr. Sharp, "how did you?"

"Aunt heard him," said Miss Garland. "She was just going into the room when she caught a word or two, and she stayed outside and listened. You don't know what a lot she thinks of you."

Mr. Sharp's eyes opened wider than ever. "I thought she didn't like me," he said, slowly.

"Good gracious!" said Miss Garland. "Whatever could have put such an idea as that into your head? Of course, aunt isn't always going to let uncle see that she agrees with him. Still, as if anybody could help—" she murmured to herself.

"Eh?" said the young man, in a trembling voice.

"Nothing."

Miss Garland walked along with averted face; Mr. Sharp, his pulses bounding, trod on air beside her.

"I thought," he said, at last "I thought that Jack Butler was a favourite of hers?"

"Jack Butler!" said the girl, in tones of scornful surprise. "The idea! How blind men are; you're all alike, I think. You can't see two inches in front of you. She's as pleased as possible that you are coming on Wednesday; and so am—"

Mr. Sharp caught his breath. "Yes?" he murmured.

"Let's go down here," said Miss Garland quickly; "down by the river. And I'll tell you what we want you to do."

She placed her hand lightly on his arm, and Mr. Sharp, with a tremulous smile, obeyed. The smile faded gradually as he listened, and an expression of anxious astonishment took its place. He shook his head as she proceeded, and twice ventured a faint suggestion that she was only speaking in jest. Convinced at last, against his will, he walked on in silent consternation.

"But," he said at last, as Miss Garland paused for breath, "your uncle would never forgive me. He'd never let me come near the house again."

"Aunt will see to that," said the girl, confidently. "But, of course, if you don't wish to please me—"

She turned away, and Mr. Sharp, plucking up spirit, ventured to take her hand and squeeze it. A faint, a very faint, squeeze in return decided him.

"It will come all right afterwards," said Miss Garland, "especially with the hold it will give aunt over him."

"I hope so," said the young man. "If not, I shall be far—farther off than ever."

Miss Garland blushed and, turning her head, gazed steadily at the river.

"Trust me," she said at last. "Me and auntie."

Mr. Sharp said that so long as he pleased her nothing else mattered, and, in the seventh heaven of delight, paced slowly along the towpath by her side.

"And you mustn't mind what auntie and I say to you," said the girl, continuing her instructions. "We must keep up appearances, you know; and if we seem to be angry, you must remember we are only pretending."

Mr. Sharp, with a tender smile, said that he understood perfectly.

"And now I had better go," said Florrie, returning the smile. "Uncle might see us together, or somebody else might see us and tell him. Good-bye."

She shook hands and went off, stopping three times to turn and wave her hand. In a state of bewildered delight Mr. Sharp continued his stroll, rehearsing, as he went, the somewhat complicated and voluminous instructions she had given him.

By Wednesday evening he was part-perfect, and, in a state of mind divided between nervousness and exaltation, set out for Mr. Culpepper's. He found that gentleman, dressed in his best, sitting in an easy-chair with his hands folded over a fancy waistcoat of startling design, and, placing a small box of small cigars on his knees, wished him the usual "Happy Returns." The entrance of the ladies, who seemed as though they had just come off the ice, interrupted Mr. Culpepper's thanks.

"Getting spoiled, that's what I am," he remarked, playfully. "See this waistcoat? My old Aunt Elizabeth sent it this morning."

He leaned back in his chair and glanced down in warm approval. "The missis gave me a pipe, and Florrie gave me half a pound of tobacco. And I bought a bottle of port wine myself, for all of us."

He pointed to a bottle that stood on the supper-table, and, the ladies retiring to the kitchen to bring in the supper, rose and placed chairs. A piece of roast beef was placed before him, and, motioning Mr. Sharp to a seat opposite Florrie, he began to carve.

"Just a nice comfortable party," he said, genially, as he finished. "Help yourself to the ale, Bert."

Mr. Sharp, ignoring the surprise on the faces of the ladies, complied, and passed the bottle to Mr. Culpepper. They drank to each other, and again a flicker of surprise appeared on the faces of Mrs. Culpepper and her niece. Mr. Culpepper, noticing it, shook his head waggishly at Mr. Sharp.

"He drinks it as if he likes it," he remarked.

"I do," asserted Mr. Sharp, and, raising his glass, emptied it, and resumed the attack on his plate. Mr. Culpepper unscrewed the top of another bottle, and the reckless Mr. Sharp, after helping himself, made a short and feeling speech, in which he wished Mr. Culpepper long life and happiness. "If you ain't happy with Mrs. Culpepper," he concluded, gallantly, "you ought to be."

Mr. Culpepper nodded and went on eating in silence until, the keen edge of his appetite having been taken off, he put down his knife and fork and waxed sentimental.

"Been married over thirty years," he said, slowly, with a glance at his wife, "and never regretted it."

"Who hasn't?" inquired Mr. Sharp.

"Why, me," returned the surprised Mr. Culpepper.

Mr. Sharp, who had just raised his glass, put it down again and smiled. It was a faint smile, but it seemed to affect his host unfavourably.

"What are you smiling at?" he demanded.

"Thoughts," said Mr. Sharp, exchanging a covert glance with Florrie. "Something you told me the other day."

Mr. Culpepper looked bewildered. "I'll give you a penny for them thoughts," he said, with an air of jocosity.

Mr. Sharp shook his head. "Money couldn't buy 'em," he said, with owlish solemnity, "espec— especially after the good supper you're giving me."

"Bert," said Mr. Culpepper, uneasily, as his wife sat somewhat erect "Bert, it's my birthday, and I don't grudge nothing to nobody; but go easy with the beer. You ain't used to it, you know."

"What's the matter with the beer?" inquired Mr. Sharp. "It tastes all right—what there is of it."

"It ain't the beer; it's you," explained Mr. Culpepper.

Mr. Sharp stared at him. "Have I said anything I oughtn't to?" he inquired.

Mr. Culpepper shook his head, and, taking up a fork and spoon, began to serve a plum-pudding that Miss Garland had just placed on the table.

"What was it you said I was to be sure and not tell Mrs. Culpepper?" inquired Mr. Sharp, dreamily. "I haven't said that, have I?"

"No!" snapped the harassed Mr. Culpepper, laying down the fork and spoon and regarding him ferociously. "I mean, there wasn't anything. I mean, I didn't say so. You're raving."

"If I did say it, I'm sorry," persisted Mr. Sharp. "I can't say fairer than that, can I?"

"You're all right," said Mr. Culpepper, trying, but in vain, to exchange a waggish glance with his wife.

"I didn't say it?" inquired Mr. Sharp.

"No," said Mr. Culpepper, still smiling in a wooden fashion.

"I mean the other thing?" said Mr. Sharp, in a thrilling whisper.

"Look here," exclaimed the overwrought Mr. Culpepper; "why not eat your pudding, and leave off talking nonsense? Nobody's listening to you."

"Speak for yourself," said his wife, tartly. "I like to hear Mr. Sharp talk. What was it he told you not to tell me?"

Mr. Sharp eyed her mistily. "I—I can't tell you," he said, slowly.

"Why not?" asked Mrs. Culpepper, coaxingly.

"Because it—it would make your hair stand on end," said the industrious Mr. Sharp.

"Nonsense," said Mrs. Culpepper, sharply.

"He said it would," said Mr. Sharp, indicating his host with his spoon, "and he ought—to know—Who's that kicking me under the table?"

Mr. Culpepper, shivering with wrath and dread, struggled for speech. "You'd better get home, Bert," he said at last. "You're not yourself. There's nobody kicking you under the table. You don't know what you are saying. You've been dreaming things. I never said anything of the kind."

"Memory's gone," said Mr. Sharp, shaking his head at him. "Clean gone. Don't you remember—"

"NO!" roared Mr. Culpepper.

Mr. Sharp sat blinking at him, but his misgivings vanished before the glances of admiring devotion which Miss Garland was sending in his direction. He construed them rightly not only as a reward, but as an incentive to further efforts. In the midst of an impressive silence Mrs. Culpepper collected the plates and, producing a dish of fruit from the sideboard, placed it upon the table.

"Help yourself, Mr. Sharp," she said, pushing the bottle of port towards him.

Mr. Sharp complied, having first, after several refusals, put a little into the ladies' glasses, and a lot on the tablecloth near Mr. Culpepper. Then, after a satisfying sip or two, he rose with a bland smile and announced his intention of making a speech.

"But you've made one," said his host, in tones of fierce expostulation.

"That—that was las' night," said Mr. Sharp. "This is to-night—your birthday."

"Well, we don't want any more," said Mr. Culpepper.

Mr. Sharp hesitated. "It's only his fun," he said, looking round and raising his glass. "He's afraid I'm going to praise him up—praise him up. Here's to my old friend, Mr. Culpepper: one of the best. We all have our—faults, and he has his—has his. Where was I?"

"Sit down," growled Mr. Culpepper.

"Talking about my husband's faults," said his wife.

"So I was," said Mr. Sharp, putting his hand to his brow. "Don't be alarm'," he continued, turning to his host; "nothing to be alarm' about. I'm not going to talk about 'em. Not so silly as that, I hope. I don't want spoil your life."

"Sit down," repeated Mr. Culpepper.

"You're very anxious he should sit down," said his wife, sharply.

"No, I'm not," said Mr. Culpepper; "only he's talking nonsense."

Mr. Sharp, still on his legs, took another sip of port and, avoiding the eye of Mr. Culpepper, which was showing signs of incipient inflammation, looked for encouragement to Miss Garland.

"He's a man we all look up to and respect," he continued. "If he does go off to London every now and then on business, that's his lookout. My idea is he always ought to take Mrs. Culpepper with him.

"He'd have pleasure of her company and, same time, he'd be money in pocket by it. And why shouldn't she go to music-halls sometimes? Why shouldn't she—"

"You get off home," said the purple Mr. Culpepper, rising and hammering the table with his fist. "Get off home; and if you so much as show your face inside this 'ouse again there'll be trouble. Go on. Out you go!"

"Home?" repeated Mr. Sharp, sitting down suddenly. "Won't go home till morning."

"Oh, we'll soon see about that," said Mr. Culpepper, taking him by the shoulders. "Come on, now."

Mr. Sharp subsided lumpishly into his chair, and Mr. Culpepper, despite his utmost efforts, failed to move him. The two ladies exchanged a glance, and then, with their heads in the air, sailed out of the room, the younger pausing at the door to bestow a mirthful glance upon Mr. Sharp ere she disappeared.

"Come—out," said Mr. Culpepper, panting.

"You trying to tickle me?" inquired Mr. Sharp.

"You get off home," said the other. "You've been doing nothing but make mischief ever since you came in. What put such things into your silly head I don't know. I shall never hear the end of 'em as long as I live."

"Silly head?" repeated Mr. Sharp, with an alarming change of manner. "Say it again."

Mr. Culpepper repeated it with gusto.

"Very good," said Mr. Sharp. He seized him suddenly and, pushing him backwards into his easychair, stood over him with such hideous contortions of visage that Mr. Culpepper was horrified. "Now you sit there and keep quite still," he said, with smouldering ferocity. "Where did you put carving-knife? Eh? Where's carving-knife?"

"No, no, Bert," said Mr. Culpepper, clutching at his sleeve. "I—I was only joking. You—you ain't quite yourself, Bert."

"What?" demanded the other, rolling his eyes, and clenching his fists.

"I—I mean you've improved," said Mr. Culpepper, hurriedly. "Wonderful, you have."

Mr. Sharp's countenance cleared a little. "Let's make a night of it," he said. "Don't move, whatever you do."

He closed the door and, putting the wine and a couple of glasses on the mantelpiece, took a chair by Mr. Culpepper and prepared to spend the evening. His instructions were too specific to be disregarded, and three times he placed his arm about the waist of the frenzied Mr. Culpepper and took him for a lumbering dance up and down the room. In the intervals between dances he regaled him with interminable extracts from speeches made at the debating society and recitations learned at school. Suggestions relating to bed, thrown out by Mr. Culpepper from time to time, were repelled with scorn. And twice, in deference to Mr. Sharp's desires, he had to join in the chorus of a song.

Ten o'clock passed, and the hands of the clock crawled round to eleven. The hour struck, and, as though in answer, the door opened and the agreeable face of Florrie Garland appeared. Behind her, to the intense surprise of both gentlemen, loomed the stalwart figure of Mr. Jack Butler.

"I thought he might be useful, uncle," said Miss Garland, coming into the room. "Auntie wouldn't let me come down before."

Mr. Sharp rose in a dazed fashion and saw Mr. Culpepper grasp Mr. Butler by the hand. More dazed still, he felt the large and clumsy hand of Mr. Butler take him by the collar and propel him with some violence along the small passage, while another hand, which he dimly recognized as belonging to Mr. Culpepper, was inserted in the small of his back. Then the front door opened and he was thrust out into the night. The door closed, and a low feminine laugh sounded from a window above.

EASY MONEY

A lad of about twenty stepped ashore from the schooner Jane, and joining a girl, who had been avoiding for some ten minutes the ardent gaze of the night-watchman, set off arm-in-arm. The watchman rolled his eyes and shook his head slowly.

Nearly all his money on 'is back, he said, and what little bit 'e's got over he'll spend on 'er. And three months arter they're married he'll wonder wot 'e ever saw in her. If a man marries he wishes he 'adn't, and if he doesn't marry he wishes he 'ad. That's life.

Looking at them two young fools reminds me of a nevy of Sam Small's; a man I think I've spoke to you of afore. As a rule Sam didn't talk much about 'is relations, but there was a sister of 'is in the country wot 'e was rather fond of because 'e 'adn't seen 'er for twenty years. She 'ad got a boy wot 'ad just got a job in London, and when 'e wrote and told 'er he was keeping company with the handsomest and loveliest and best 'arted gal in the whole wide world, she wrote to Sam about it and asked im to give 'is nevy some good advice.

Sam 'ad just got back from China and was living with Peter Russet and Ginger Dick as usual, and arter reading the letter about seven times and asking Ginger how 'e spelt "minx," 'e read the letter out loud to them and asked 'em what they thought about it.

Ginger shook his 'ead, and, arter thinking a bit, Peter shook his too.

"She's caught 'im rather young," ses Ginger.

"They get it bad at that age too," ses Peter. "When I was twenty, there was a gal as I was fond of, and a regiment couldn't ha' parted us."

"Wot did part you then?" ses Sam.

"Another gal," ses Peter; "a gal I took a fancy to, that's wot did it."

"I was nearly married when I was twenty," ses Ginger, with a far-away look in his eyes. "She was the most beautiful gal I ever saw in my life; she 'ad one 'undred pounds a year of 'er own and she couldn't bear me out of her sight. If a thump acrost the chest would do that cough of yours any good, Sam—"

"Don't take no notice of 'im, Ginger," ses Peter. "Why didn't you marry 'er?"

"'Cos I was afraid she might think I was arter 'er money," ses Ginger, getting a little bit closer to Sam.

Peter 'ad another turn then, and him and Ginger kept on talking about gals whose 'arts they 'ad broke till Sam didn't know what to do with 'imself.

"I'll just step round and see my nevy, while you and Peter are amusing each other," he ses at last. "I'll ask 'im to come round to-morrow and then you can give 'im good advice."

The nevy came round next evening. Bright, cheerful young chap 'e was, and he agreed with everything they said. When Peter said as 'ow all gals was deceivers, he said he'd known it for years, but they was born that way and couldn't 'elp it; and when Ginger said that no man ought to marry afore he was fifty, he corrected 'im and made it fifty-five.

"I'm glad to 'ear you talk like that," ses Ginger.

"So am I," ses Peter.

"He's got his 'ead screwed on right," ses Sam, wot thought his sister 'ad made a mistake.

"I'm surprised when I look round at the wimmen men 'ave married," ses the nevy; "wot they could 'ave seen in them I can't think. Me and my young lady often laugh about it."

"Your wot?" ses Sam, pretending to be very surprised.

"My young lady," ses the nevy.

Sam gives a cough. "I didn't know you'd got a young lady," he ses.

"Well, I 'ave," ses his nevy, "and we're going to be married at Christmas."

"But—but you ain't fifty-five," ses Ginger.

"I'm twenty-one," ses the nevy, "but my case is different. There isn't another young lady like mine in the world. She's different to all the others, and it ain't likely I'm going to let 'er be snapped up by somebody else. Fifty-five! Why, 'ow I'm to wait till Christmas I don't know. She's the prettiest and handsomest gal in the world; and she's the cleverest one I ever met. You ought to hear 'er laugh. Like music it is. You'd never forget it."

"Twenty-one is young," ses Ginger, shaking his 'ead. "'Ave you known 'er long?"

"Three months," ses the nevy. "She lives in the same street as I do. 'Ow it is she ain't been snapped up before, I can't think, but she told me that she didn't care for men till she saw me."

"They all say that," ses Ginger.

"If I've 'ad it said to me once, I've 'ad it said twenty times," ses Peter, nodding.

"They do it to flatter," ses old Sam, looking as if 'e knew all about it. "You wait till you are my age, Joe; then you'll know; why I should ha' been married dozens o' times if I 'adn't been careful."

"P'r'aps it was a bit on both sides," ses Joe, looking at 'is uncle. "P'r'aps they was careful too. If you only saw my young lady, you wouldn't talk like that. She's got the truthfullest eyes in the world. Large grey eyes like a child's, leastways sometimes they are grey and sometimes they are blue. It seems to depend on the light somehow; I 'ave seen them when they was a brown-brownish-gold. And she smiles with 'er eyes."

"Hasn't she got a mouth?" ses Ginger, wot was getting a bit tired of it.

"You've been crossed in love," ses the nevy, staring at 'im. "That's wot's the matter with you. And looking at you, I don't wonder at it."

Ginger 'arf got up, but Sam gave him a look and 'e sat down agin, and then they all sat quiet while the nevy went on telling them about 'is gal.

"I should like to see 'er," ses his uncle at last.

"Call round for me at seven to-morrow night," ses the young 'un, "and I'll introduce you."

"We might look in on our way," ses Sam, arter Ginger and Peter 'ad both made eyes at 'im. "We're going out to spend the evening."

"The more the merrier," ses his nevy. "Well, so long; I expect she's waiting for me."

He got up and said good-bye, and arter he 'ad gorn, Sam and the other two shook their leads together and said what a pity it was to be twenty-one. Ginger said it made 'im sad to think of it, and Peter said 'ow any gal could look at a man under thirty, 'e couldn't think.

They all went round to the nevy's the next evening. They was a little bit early owing to Ginger's watch 'aving been set right by guess-work, and they 'ad to sit in a row on the nevy's bed waiting while e cleaned 'imself, and changed his clothes. Although it was only Wednesday 'e changed his collar, and he was so long making up 'is mind about his necktie that 'is uncle tried to make it up for him. By the time he 'ad finished Sam said it made 'im think it was Sunday.

Miss Gill was at 'ome when they got there, and all three of 'em was very much surprised that such a good-looking gal should take up with Sam's nevy. Ginger nearly said so, but Peter gave 'im a dig in the back just in time and 'e called him something under 'is breath instead.

"Why shouldn't we all make an evening of it?" ses Ginger, arter they 'ad been talking for about ten minutes, and the nevy 'ad looked at the clock three or four times.

"Because two's company," ses Mrs. Gill. "Why you was young yourself once. Can't you remember?"

"He's young now, mother," ses the gal, giving Ginger a nice smile.

"I tell you wot we might do," ses Mrs. Gill, putting 'er finger to her forehead and considering. "You and Joe go out and 'ave your evening, and me and these gentlemen'll go off together somewhere. I shall enjoy an outing; I ain't 'ad one for a long time."

Ginger said it would be very nice if she thought it wouldn't make 'er too tired, and afore Sam or Peter could think of anything to say, she was upstairs putting 'er bonnet on. They thought o' plenty to say while they was sitting alone with Ginger waiting for 'er.

"My idea was for the gal and your nevy to come too," ses pore Ginger. "Then I thought we might lose 'im and I would 'ave a little chat with the gal, and show 'er 'ow foolish she was."

"Well, you've done it now," ses Sam. "Spoilt our evening."

"P'r'aps good will come out of it," ses Ginger. "If the old lady takes a fancy to us we shall be able to come agin, and then to please you, Sam, I'll have a go to cut your nevy out."

Sam stared at 'im, and Peter stared too, and then they looked at each other and began to laugh till Ginger forgot where 'e was and offered to put Sam through the winder. They was still quarrelling under their breath and saying wot they'd like to do to each other when Mrs. Gill came downstairs. Dressed up to the nines she was, and they walked down the street with a feeling that everybody was looking at em.

One thing that 'elped to spoil the evening was that Mrs. Gill wouldn't go into public'ouses, but to make up for it she went into sweet-stuff shops three times and 'ad ices while they stood and watched 'er and wondered 'ow she could do it. And arter that she stopped at a place Poplar way, where there was a few swings and roundabouts and things. She was as skittish as a school-gal, and arter taking pore Sam on the roundabout till 'e didn't know whether he was on his 'eels or his 'ead, she got 'im into a boat-swing and swung 'im till he felt like a boy on 'is fust v'y'ge. Arter that she took 'im to the rifle gallery, and afore he had 'ad three shots the man took the gun away from 'im and threatened to send for the police.

It was an expensive evening for all of them, but as Ginger said when they got 'ome they 'ad broken the ice, and he bet Peter Russet 'arf a dollar that afore two days 'ad passed he'd take the nevy's gal for a walk. He stepped round by 'imself the next arternoon and made 'imself agreeable to Mrs. Gill, and the day arter they was both so nice and kind that 'e plucked up 'is courage and offered to take Miss Gill to the Zoo.

She said "No" at fust, of course, but arter Ginger 'ad pointed out that Joe was at work all day and couldn't take 'er 'imself, and that 'e was Joe's uncle's best pal, she began to think better of it.

"Why not?" ses her mother. "Joe wouldn't mind. He wouldn't be so silly as to be jealous o' Mr. Ginger Dick."

"Of course not," ses the gal. "There's nothing to be jealous of."

She let 'er mother and Ginger persuade 'er arter a time, and then she went upstairs to clean herself, and put on a little silver brooch that Ginger said he 'ad picked up coming along.

She took about three-quarters of an hour to get ready, but when she came down, Ginger felt that it was quite worth it. He couldn't take 'is eyes off 'er, as the saying goes, and 'e sat by 'er side on the top of the omnibus like a man in a dream.

"This is better than being at sea," he ses at last.

"Don't you like the sea?" ses the gal. "I should like to go to sea myself."

"I shouldn't mind the sea if you was there," ses Ginger.

Miss Gill turned her 'ead away. "You mustn't talk to me like that," she ses in a soft voice. "Still—"

"Still wot?" ses Ginger, arter waiting a long time.

"I mean, if I did go to sea, it would be nice to have a friend on board," she ses. "I suppose you ain't afraid of storms, are you?"

"I like 'em," ses Ginger.

"You look as if you would," ses the gal, giving 'im a little look under 'er eyelashes. "It must be nice to be a man and be brave. I wish I was a man."

"I don't," ses Ginger.

"Why not?" ses the gal, turning her 'ead away agin.

Ginger didn't answer, he gave 'er elbow a little squeeze instead. She took it away at once, and Ginger was just wishing he 'adn't been so foolish, when it came back agin, and they sat for a long time without speaking a word.

"The sea is all right for some things," ses Ginger at last, "but suppose a man married!"

The gal shook her 'ead. "It would be hard on 'is wife," she ses, with another little look at 'im, "but— but—"

Ginger pinched 'er elbow agin.

"But p'r'aps he could get a job ashore," she ses, "and then he could take his wife out for a bus-ride every day."

They 'ad to change buses arter a time, and they got on a wrong bus and went miles out o' their way, but neither of 'em seemed to mind. Ginger said he was thinking of something else, and the gal said she was too. They got to the Zoological Gardens at last, and Ginger said he 'ad never enjoyed himself so much. When the lions roared she squeezed his arm, and when they 'ad an elephant ride she was holding on to 'im with both 'ands.

"I am enjoying myself," she ses, as Ginger 'elped her down and said "whoa" to the elephant. "I know it's wicked, but I can't 'elp it, and wot's more, I'm afraid I don't want to 'elp it."

She let Ginger take 'er arm when she nearly tripped up over a peppermint ball some kid 'ad dropped; and, arter a little persuasion, she 'ad a bottle of lemonade and six bath-buns at a refreshment stall for dinner.

She was as nice as she could be to him, but by the time they started for 'ome, she 'ad turned so quiet that Ginger began to think 'e must 'ave offended 'er in some way.

"Are you tired?" he ses.

"No," ses the gal, shaking her 'ead, "I've enjoyed myself very much."

"I thought you seemed a bit tired," ses Ginger, arter waiting a long time.

"I'm not tired," ses the gal, giving 'im a sad sort o' little smile, "but I'm a little bit worried, that's all."

"Worried?" ses Ginger, very tender. "Wot's worrying you?"

"Oh, I can't tell you," ses Miss Gill. "It doesn't matter; I'll try and cheer up. Wot a lovely day it is, isn't it? I shall remember it all my life."

"Wot is it worrying you?" ses Ginger, in a determined voice. "Can't you tell me?"

"No," ses the gal, shaking her 'ead, "I can't tell you because you might want to 'elp me, and I couldn't allow that."

"Why shouldn't I 'elp you?" ses Ginger. "It's wot we was put 'ere for: to 'elp one another."

"I couldn't tell you," ses the gal, just dabbing at'er eyes—with a lace pocket-'ankercher about one and a 'arf times the size of 'er nose.

"Not if I ask you to?" ses Ginger.

Miss Gill shook 'er 'ead, and then she tried her 'ardest to turn the conversation. She talked about the weather, and the monkey-'ouse, and a gal in 'er street whose 'air changed from red to black in a single night; but it was all no good, Ginger wouldn't be put off, and at last she ses—

"Well," she ses, "if you must know, I'm in a difficulty; I 'ave got to get three pounds, and where to get it I don't know any more than the man in the moon. Now let's talk about something else."

"Do you owe it?" ses Ginger.

"I can't tell you anymore," ses Miss Gill, "and I wouldn't 'ave told you that only you asked me, and somehow I feel as though I 'ave to tell you things, when you want me to."

"Three pounds ain't much," ses pore Ginger, wot 'ad just been paid off arter a long v'y'ge. "I can let you 'ave it and welcome."

Miss Gill started away from 'im as though she 'ad been stung, and it took 'im all his time to talk 'er round agin. When he 'ad she begged 'is pardon and said he was the most generous man she 'ad ever met, but it couldn't be.

"I don't know when I could pay it back," she ses, "but I thank you all the same for offering it."

"Pay it back when you like," ses Ginger, "and if you never pay it back, it don't matter."

He offered 'er the money four or five times, but she wouldn't take it, but at last just as they got near her 'ouse he forced it in her 'and, and put his own 'ands in his pockets when she tried to make 'im take it back.

"You are good to me," she ses arter they 'ad gone inside and 'er mother 'ad gone upstairs arter giving Ginger a bottle o' beer to amuse 'imself with; "I shall never forget you. Never."

"I 'ope not," ses Ginger, starting. "Are you coming out agin to-morrow?"

"I'm afraid I can't," ses Miss Gill, shaking her 'ead and looking sorrowful.

"Not with me?" ses Ginger, sitting down beside her on the sofa and putting 'is arm so that she could lean against it if she wanted to.

"I don't think I can," ses the gal, leaning back very gentle.

"Think agin," ses Ginger, squeezing 'er waist a little.

Miss Gill shook her 'ead, and then turned and looked at 'im. Her face was so close to his, that, thinking that she 'ad put it there a-purpose, he kissed it, and the next moment 'e got a clout that made his 'ead ring.

"'Ow dare you!" she ses, jumping up with a scream. "'Ow dare you! 'Ow dare—"

"Wot's the matter?" ses her mother, coming downstairs like a runaway barrel of treacle.

"He—he's insulted me," ses Miss Gill, taking out her little 'ankercher and sobbing. "He—k-kissed me!"

"WOT!" ses Mrs. Gill. "Well, I'd never 'ave believed it! Never! Why 'e ought to be taken up. Wot d'ye mean by it?" she ses, turning on pore Ginger.

Ginger tried to explain, but it was all no good, and two minutes arterwards 'e was walking back to 'is lodgings like a dog with its tail between its legs. His 'ead was going round and round with astonishment, and 'e was in such a temper that 'e barged into a man twice as big as himself and then offered to knock his 'ead off when 'e objected. And when Sam and Peter asked him 'ow he 'ad got on, he was in such a state of mind it was all 'e could do to answer 'em.

"And I'll trouble you for my 'arf dollar, Peter," he ses; "I've been out with 'er all day, and I've won my bet."

Peter paid it over like a lamb, and then 'e sat thinking 'ard for a bit.

"Are you going out with 'er agin to-morrow, Ginger?" he ses, arter a time.

"I don't know," ses Ginger, careless-like, "I ain't made up my mind yet."

Peter looked at 'im and then 'e looked at Sam and winked. "Let me 'ave a try," he ses; "I'll bet you another 'arf dollar that I take 'er out. P'r'aps I shall come 'ome in a better temper than wot you 'ave."

Old Sam said it wasn't right to play with a gal's 'art in that way, but arter a lot o' talking and telling Sam to shut up, Ginger took the bet. He was quite certain in his own mind that Miss Gill would slam the door in Peter's face, and arter he 'ad started off next morning, Ginger and Sam waited in to 'ave the pleasure of laughing in 'is face.

They got tired of waiting at last, and went out to enjoy themselves, and breathe the fresh air in a pub down Poplar way. They got back at seven o'clock, and ten minutes arterwards Peter came in and sat down on his bed and began to smoke without a word.

"Had a good time?" ses Ginger.

"Rippin'," ses Peter, holding 'is pipe tight between 'is teeth. "You owe me 'arf a dollar, Ginger."

"Where'd you go?" ses Ginger, passing it over.

"Crystal Pallis," ses Peter.

"Are you going to take 'er out to-morrow?" ses Sam.

"I don't think so," ses Peter, taking 'is pipe out of 'is mouth and yawning. "She's rather too young for me; I like talking to gals wot's a bit older. I won't stand in Ginger's way."

"I found 'er a bit young too," ses Ginger. "P'r'aps we'd better let Sam's nevy 'ave 'er. Arter all it's a bit rough on 'im when you come to think of it."

"You're quite right," ses Peter, jumping up. "It's Sam's business, and why we should go out of our way and inconvenience ourselves to do 'im a good turn, I don't know."

"It's Sam all over," ses Ginger; "he's always been like that, and the more you try to oblige 'im, the more you may."

They went on abusing Sam till he got sick and tired of it, and arter telling 'em wot he thought of 'em he slammed the door and went out and spent the evening by 'imself. He would 'ardly speak to them next day, but arter tea he brightened up a bit and they went off together as if nothing 'ad happened, and the fust thing they saw as they turned out of their street was Sam's nevy coming along smiling till it made their faces ache to look at him.

"I was just coming to see you," he ses.

"We're just off on business," ses Ginger.

"I wasn't going to stop," ses the nevy; "my young lady just told me to step along and show uncle wot she has bought me. A silver watch and chain and a gold ring. Look at it!"

He held his 'and under Ginger's nose, and Ginger stood there looking at it and opening and shutting 'is mouth like a dying fish. Then he took Peter by the arm and led 'im away while the nevy was opening 'is new watch and showing Sam the works.

"'Ow much did she get out of you, Peter?" ses Ginger, looking at 'im very hard. "I don't want any lies."

"Three quid," ses Peter, staring at 'im.

"Same 'ere," ses Ginger, grinding his teeth. "Did she give you a smack on the side of your face?"

"Wot—are—you—talking about, Ginger?" ses Peter.

"Did she smack your face too?" ses Ginger.

"Yes," ses Peter.

ESTABLISHING RELATIONS

Mr. Richard Catesby, second officer of the ss. *Wizard*, emerged from the dock-gates in high good-humour to spend an evening ashore. The bustle of the day had departed, and the inhabitants of Wapping, in search of coolness and fresh air, were sitting at open doors and windows indulging in general conversation with any-body within earshot.

Mr. Catesby, turning into Bashford's Lane, lost in a moment all this life and colour. The hum of distant voices certainly reached there, but that was all, for Bashford's Lane, a retiring thoroughfare facing a blank dock wall, capped here and there by towering spars, set an example of gentility which neighbouring streets had long ago decided crossly was impossible for ordinary people to follow. Its neatly grained shutters, fastened back by the sides of the windows, gave a pleasing idea of uniformity, while its white steps and polished brass knockers were suggestive of almost a Dutch cleanliness.

Mr. Catesby, strolling comfortably along, stopped suddenly for another look at a girl who was standing in the ground-floor window of No. 5. He went on a few paces and then walked back slowly, trying to look as though he had forgotten something. The girl was still there, and met his ardent glances unmoved: a fine girl, with large, dark eyes, and a complexion which was the subject of much scandalous discussion among neighbouring matrons.

"It must be something wrong with the glass, or else it's the bad light," said Mr. Catesby to himself; "no girl is so beautiful as that."

He went by again to make sure. The object of his solicitude was still there and apparently unconscious of his existence. He passed very slowly and sighed deeply.

"You've got it at last, Dick Catesby," he said, solemnly; "fair and square in the most dangerous part of the heart. It's serious this time."

He stood still on the narrow pavement, pondering, and then, in excuse of his flagrant misbehaviour, murmured, "It was meant to be," and went by again. This time he fancied that he detected a somewhat supercilious expression in the dark eyes—a faint raising of well-arched eyebrows.

His engagement to wait at Aldgate Station for the second-engineer and spend an evening together was dismissed as too slow to be considered. He stood for some time in uncertainty, and then turning slowly into the Beehive, which stood at the corner, went into the private bar and ordered a glass of beer.

He was the only person in the bar, and the land-lord, a stout man in his shirt-sleeves, was the soul of affability. Mr. Catesby, after various general remarks, made a few inquiries about an uncle aged five minutes, whom he thought was living in Bashford's Lane.

"I don't know 'im," said the landlord.

"I had an idea that he lived at No. 5," said Catesby.

The landlord shook his head. "That's Mrs. Truefitt's house," he said, slowly.

Mr. Catesby pondered. "Truefitt, Truefitt," he repeated; "what sort of a woman is she?"

"Widder-woman," said the landlord; "she lives there with 'er daughter Prudence."

Mr. Catesby said "Indeed!" and being a good listener learned that Mrs. Truefitt was the widow of a master-lighterman, and that her son, Fred Truefitt, after an absence of seven years in New Zealand, was now on his way home. He finished his glass slowly and, the landlord departing to attend to another customer, made his way into the street again.

He walked along slowly, picturing as he went the home-corning of the long-absent son. Things were oddly ordered in this world, and Fred Truefitt would probably think nothing of his brotherly privileges. He wondered whether he was like Prudence. He wondered—

"By Jove, I'll do it!" he said, recklessly, as he turned. "Now for a row."

He walked back rapidly to Bashford's Lane, and without giving his courage time to cool plied the knocker of No. 5 briskly.

The door was opened by an elderly woman, thin, and somewhat querulous in expression. Mr. Catesby had just time to notice this, and then he flung his arm round her waist, and hailing her as "Mother!" saluted her warmly.

The faint scream of the astounded Mrs. Truefitt brought her daughter hastily into the passage. Mr. Catesby's idea was ever to do a thing thoroughly, and, relinquishing Mrs. Truefitt, he kissed Prudence with all the ardour which a seven-years' absence might be supposed to engender in the heart of a devoted brother. In return he received a box on the ears which made his head ring.

"He's been drinking," gasped the dismayed Mrs. Truefitt.

"Don't you know me, mother?" inquired Mr. Richard Catesby, in grievous astonishment.

"He's mad," said her daughter.

"Am I so altered that you don't know me, Prudence?" inquired Mr. Catesby; with pathos. "Don't you know your Fred?"

"Go out," said Mrs. Truefitt, recovering; "go out at once."

Mr. Catesby looked from one to the other in consternation.

"I know I've altered," he said, at last, "but I'd no idea—"

"If you don't go out at once I'll send for the police," said the elder woman, sharply. "Prudence, scream!"

"I'm not going to scream," said Prudence, eyeing the intruder with great composure. "I'm not afraid of him."

Despite her reluctance to have a scene—a thing which was strongly opposed to the traditions of Bashford's Lane—Mrs. Truefitt had got as far as the doorstep in search of assistance, when a sudden terrible thought occurred to her: Fred was dead, and the visitor had hit upon this extraordinary fashion of breaking the news gently.

"Come into the parlour," she said, faintly.

Mr. Catesby, suppressing his surprise, followed her into the room. Prudence, her fine figure erect and her large eyes meeting his steadily, took up a position by the side of her mother.

"You have brought bad news?" inquired the latter.

"No, mother," said Mr. Catesby, simply, "only myself, that's all."

Mrs. Truefitt made a gesture of impatience, and her daughter, watching him closely, tried to remember something she had once read about detecting insanity by the expression of the eyes. Those of Mr. Catesby were blue, and the only expression in them at the present moment was one of tender and respectful admiration.

"When did you see Fred last?" inquired Mrs. Truefitt, making another effort.

"Mother," said Mr. Catesby, with great pathos, "don't you know me?"

"He has brought bad news of Fred," said Mrs. Truefitt, turning to her daughter; "I am sure he has."

"I don't understand you," said Mr. Catesby, with a bewildered glance from one to the other. "I am Fred. Am I much changed? You look the same as you always did, and it seems only yesterday since I kissed Prudence good-bye at the docks. You were crying, Prudence."

Miss Truefitt made no reply; she gazed at him unflinchingly and then bent toward her mother.

"He is mad," she whispered; "we must try and get him out quietly. Don't contradict him."

"Keep close to me," said Mrs. Truefitt, who had a great horror of the insane. "If he turns violent open the window and scream. I thought he had brought bad news of Fred. How did he know about him?"

Her daughter shook her head and gazed curiously at their afflicted visitor. She put his age down at twenty-five, and she could not help thinking it a pity that so good-looking a young man should have lost his wits.

"Bade Prudence good-bye at the docks," continued Mr. Catesby, dreamily. "You drew me behind a pile of luggage, Prudence, and put your head on my shoulder. I have thought of it ever since."

Miss Truefitt did not deny it, but she bit her lips, and shot a sharp glance at him. She began to think that her pity was uncalled-for.

"I'm just going as far as the corner."

"Tell me all that's happened since I've been away," said Mr. Catesby.

Mrs. Truefitt turned to her daughter and whispered. It might have been merely the effect of a guilty conscience, but the visitor thought that he caught the word "policeman."

"I'm just going as far as the corner," said Mrs. Truefitt, rising, and crossing hastily to the door.

The young man nodded affectionately and sat in doubtful consideration as the front door closed behind her. "Where is mother going?" he asked, in a voice which betrayed a little pardonable anxiety.

"Not far, I hope," said Prudence.

"I really think," said Mr. Catesby, rising—"I really think that I had better go after her. At her age—"

He walked into the small passage and put his hand on the latch. Prudence, now quite certain of his sanity, felt sorely reluctant to let such impudence go unpunished.

"Are you going?" she inquired.

"I think I'd better," said Mr. Catesby, gravely. "Dear mother—"

"You're afraid," said the girl, calmly.

Mr. Catesby coloured and his buoyancy failed him. He felt a little bit cheap.

"You are brave enough with two women," continued the girl, disdainfully; "but you had better go if you're afraid."

Mr. Catesby regarded the temptress uneasily. "Would you like me to stay?" he asked.

"I?" said Miss Truefitt, tossing her head. "No, I don't want you. Besides, you're frightened."

Mr. Catesby turned, and with a firm step made his way back to the room; Prudence, with a half-smile, took a chair near the door and regarded her prisoner with unholy triumph.

"I shouldn't like to be in your shoes," she said, agreeably; "mother has gone for a policeman."

"Bless her," said Mr. Catesby, fervently. "What had we better say to him when he comes?"

"You'll be locked up," said Prudence; "and it will serve you right for your bad behaviour."

Mr. Catesby sighed. "It's the heart," he said, gravely. "I'm not to blame, really. I saw you standing in the window, and I could see at once that you were beautiful, and good, and kind."

"I never heard of such impudence," continued Miss Truefitt.

"I surprised myself," admitted Mr. Catesby. "In the usual way I am very quiet and well-behaved, not to say shy."

Miss Truefitt looked at him scornfully. "I think that you had better stop your nonsense and go," she remarked.

"Don't you want me to be punished?" inquired the other, in a soft voice.

"I think that you had better go while you can," said the girl, and at that moment there was a heavy knock at the front-door. Mr. Catesby, despite his assurance, changed colour; the girl eyed him in perplexity. Then she opened the small folding-doors at the back of the room.

"You're only—stupid," she whispered. "Quick! Go in there. I'll say you've gone. Keep quiet, and I'll let you out by-and-by."

She pushed him in and closed the doors. From his hiding-place he heard an animated conversation at the street-door and minute particulars as to the time which had elapsed since his departure and the direction he had taken.

"I never heard such impudence," said Mrs. Truefitt, going into the front-room and sinking into a chair after the constable had taken his departure. "I don't believe he was mad."

"Only a little weak in the head, I think," said Prudence, in a clear voice. "He was very frightened after you had gone; I don't think he will trouble us again."

"He'd better not," said Mrs. Truefitt, sharply. "I never heard of such a thing—never."

She continued to grumble, while Prudence, in a low voice, endeavoured to soothe her. Her efforts were evidently successful, as the prisoner was, after a time, surprised to hear the older woman laugh—at first gently, and then with so much enjoyment that her daughter was at some pains to restrain her. He sat in patience until evening deepened into night, and a line of light beneath the folding-doors announced the lighting of the lamp in the front-room. By a pleasant clatter of crockery he became aware that they were at supper, and he pricked up his ears as Prudence made another reference to him.

"If he comes to-morrow night while you are out I sha'n't open the door," she said. "You'll be back by nine, I suppose."

Mrs. Truefitt assented.

"And you won't be leaving before seven," continued Prudence. "I shall be all right."

Mr. Catesby's face glowed and his eyes grew tender; Prudence was as clever as she was beautiful. The delicacy with which she had intimated the fact of the unconscious Mrs. Truefitt's absence on the following evening was beyond all praise. The only depressing thought was that such resourcefulness savoured of practice.

He sat in the darkness for so long that even the proximity of Prudence was not sufficient amends for the monotony of it, and it was not until past ten o'clock that the folding-doors were opened and he stood blinking at the girl in the glare of the lamp.

"Quick!" she whispered.

Mr. Catesby stepped into the lighted room.

"The front-door is open," whispered Prudence. "Make haste. I'll close it."

She followed him to the door; he made an ineffectual attempt to seize her hand, and the next moment was pushed gently outside and the door closed behind him. He stood a moment gazing at the house, and then hastened back to his ship.

"Seven to-morrow," he murmured; "seven to-morrow. After all, there's nothing pays in this world like cheek—nothing."

He slept soundly that night, though the things that the second-engineer said to him about wasting a hard-working man's evening would have lain heavy on the conscience of a more scrupulous man. The only thing that troubled him was the manifest intention of his friend not to let him slip through his fingers on the following evening. At last, in sheer despair at his inability to shake him off, he had to tell him that he had an appointment with a lady.

"Well, I'll come, too," said the other, glowering at him. "It's very like she'll have a friend with her; they generally do."

"I'll run round and tell her," said Catesby. "I'd have arranged it before, only I thought you didn't care about that sort of thing."

"Female society is softening," said the second-engineer. "I'll go and put on a clean collar."

Catesby watched him into his cabin and then, though it still wanted an hour to seven, hastily quitted the ship and secreted himself in the private bar of the Beehive.

He waited there until a quarter past seven, and then, adjusting his tie for about the tenth time that evening in the glass behind the bar, sallied out in the direction of No. 5.

He knocked lightly, and waited. There was no response, and he knocked again. When the fourth knock brought no response, his heart sank within him and he indulged in vain speculations as to the reasons for this unexpected hitch in the programme. He knocked again, and then the door opened suddenly and Prudence, with a little cry of surprise and dismay, backed into the passage.

"You!" she said, regarding him with large eyes. Mr. Catesby bowed tenderly, and passing in closed the door behind him.

"I wanted to thank you for your kindness last night," he said, humbly.

"Very well," said Prudence; "good-bye."

Mr. Catesby smiled. "It'll take me a long time to thank you as I ought to thank you," he murmured. "And then I want to apologise; that'll take time, too."

"You had better go," said Prudence, severely; "kindness is thrown away upon you. I ought to have let you be punished."

"You are too good and kind," said the other, drifting by easy stages into the parlour.

Miss Truefitt made no reply, but following him into the room seated herself in an easy-chair and sat coldly watchful.

"How do you know what I am?" she inquired.

"Your face tells me," said the infatuated Richard. "I hope you will forgive me for my rudeness last night. It was all done on the spur of the moment."

"I am glad you are sorry," said the girl, softening.

"All the same, if I hadn't done it," pursued Mr. Catesby, "I shouldn't be sitting here talking to you now."

Miss Truefitt raised her eyes to his, and then lowered them modestly to the ground. "That is true," she said, quietly.

"And I would sooner be sitting here than any-where," pursued Catesby. "That is," he added, rising, and taking a chair by her side, "except here."

Miss Truefitt appeared to tremble, and made as though to rise. Then she sat still and took a gentle peep at Mr. Catesby from the corner of her eye.

"I hope that you are not sorry that I am here?" said that gentleman.

Miss Truefitt hesitated. "No," she said, at last."

"Are you—are you glad?" asked the modest Richard.

Miss Truefitt averted her eyes altogether. "Yes," she said, faintly.

A strange feeling of solemnity came over the triumphant Richard. He took the hand nearest to him and pressed it gently.

"I—I can hardly believe in my good luck," he murmured.

"Good luck?" said Prudence, innocently.

"Isn't it good luck to hear you say that you are glad I'm here?" said Catesby.

"You're the best judge of that," said the girl, withdrawing her hand. "It doesn't seem to me much to be pleased about."

Mr. Catesby eyed her in perplexity, and was about to address another tender remark to her when she was overcome by a slight fit of coughing. At the same moment he started at the sound of a shuffling footstep in the passage. Somebody tapped at the door.

"Yes?" said Prudence.

"Can't find the knife-powder, miss," said a harsh voice. The door was pushed open and disclosed a tall, bony woman of about forty. Her red arms were bare to the elbow, and she betrayed several evidences of a long and arduous day's charing.

"It's in the cupboard," said Prudence. "Why, what's the matter, Mrs. Porter?"

Mrs. Porter made no reply. Her mouth was wide open and she was gazing with starting eyeballs at Mr. Catesby.

"Joe!" she said, in a hoarse whisper. "Joe!"

Mr. Catesby gazed at her in chilling silence. Miss Truefitt, with an air of great surprise, glanced from one to the other.

"Joe!" said Mrs. Porter again. "Ain't you goin' to speak to me?"

Mr. Catesby continued to gaze at her in speechless astonishment. She skipped clumsily round the table and stood before him with her hands clasped.

"Where 'ave you been all this long time?" she demanded, in a higher key.

"You—you've made a mistake," said the bewildered Richard.

"Mistake?" wailed Mrs. Porter. "Mistake! Oh, where's your 'art?"

Before he could get out of her way she flung her arms round the horrified young man's neck and embraced him copiously. Over her bony left shoulder the frantic Richard met the ecstatic gaze of Miss Truefitt, and, in a flash, he realised the trap into which he had fallen.

"Mrs. Porter!" said Prudence.

"It's my 'usband, miss," said the Amazon, reluctantly releasing the flushed and dishevelled Richard; "'e left me and my five eighteen months ago. For eighteen months I 'aven't 'ad a sight of 'is blessed face."

She lifted the hem of her apron to her face and broke into discordant weeping.

"Don't cry," said Prudence, softly; "I'm sure he isn't worth it."

Mr. Catesby looked at her wanly. He was beyond further astonishment, and when Mrs. Truefitt entered the room with a laudable attempt to twist her features into an expression of surprise, he scarcely noticed her.

"It's my Joe," said Mrs. Porter, simply.

"Good gracious!" said Mrs. Truefitt. "Well, you've got him now; take care he doesn't run away from you again."

"I'll look after that, ma'am," said Mrs. Porter, with a glare at the startled Richard.

"She's very forgiving," said Prudence. "She kissed him just now."

"Did she, though," said the admiring Mrs. Truefitt. "I wish I'd been here."

"I can do it agin, ma'am," said the obliging Mrs. Porter.

"If you come near me again—" said the breathless Richard, stepping back a pace.

"I shouldn't force his love," said Mrs. Truefitt; "it'll come back in time, I dare say."

"I'm sure he's affectionate," said Prudence.

Mr. Catesby eyed his tormentors in silence; the faces of Prudence and her mother betokened much innocent enjoyment, but the austerity of Mrs. Porter's visage was unrelaxed.

"Better let bygones be bygones," said Mrs. Truefitt; "he'll be sorry by-and-by for all the trouble he has caused."

"He'll be ashamed of himself—if you give him time," added Prudence.

Mr. Catesby had heard enough; he took up his hat and crossed to the door.

"Take care he doesn't run away from you again," repeated Mrs. Truefitt.

"I'll see to that, ma'am," said Mrs. Porter, taking him by the arm. "Come along, Joe."

Mr. Catesby attempted to shake her off, but in vain, and he ground his teeth as he realised the absurdity of his position. A man he could have dealt with, but Mrs. Porter was invulnerable. Sooner than walk down the road with her he preferred the sallies of the parlour. He walked back to his old position by the fireplace, and stood gazing moodily at the floor.

Mrs. Truefitt tired of the sport at last. She wanted her supper, and with a significant glance at her daughter she beckoned the redoubtable and reluctant Mrs. Porter from the room. Catesby heard the kitchen-door close behind them, but he made no move. Prudence stood gazing at him in silence.

"If you want to go," she said, at last, "now is your chance."

Catesby followed her into the passage without a word, and waited quietly while she opened the door. Still silent, he put on his hat and passed out into the darkening street. He turned after a short distance for a last look at the house and, with a sudden sense of elation, saw that she was standing on the step. He hesitated, and then walked slowly back.

"Yes?" said Prudence.

"I should like to tell your mother that I am sorry," he said, in a low voice.

"It is getting late," said the girl, softly; "but, if you really wish to tell her—Mrs. Porter will not be here to-morrow night."

She stepped back into the house and the door closed behind her.

FAIRY GOLD

"Come and have a pint and talk it over," said Mr. Augustus Teak. "I've got reasons in my 'ead that you don't dream of, Alf."

Mr. Chase grunted and stole a side-glance at the small figure of his companion. "All brains, you are, Gussie," he remarked. "That's why it is you're so well off."

"Come and have a pint," repeated the other, and with surprising ease pushed his bulky friend into the bar of the "Ship and Anchor." Mr. Chase, mellowed by a long draught, placed his mug on the counter and eyeing him kindly, said—

"I've been in my lodgings thirteen years."

"I know," said Mr. Teak; "but I've got a partikler reason for wanting you. Our lodger, Mr. Dunn, left last week, and I only thought of you yesterday. I mentioned you to my missis, and she was quite pleased. You see, she knows I've known you for over twenty years, and she wants to make sure of only 'aving honest people in the 'ouse. She has got a reason for it."

He closed one eye and nodded with great significance at his friend.

"Oh!" said Mr. Chase, waiting.

"She's a rich woman," said Mr. Teak, pulling the other's ear down to his mouth. "She—"

"When you've done tickling me with your whiskers," said Mr. Chase, withdrawing his head and rubbing his ear vigorously, "I shall be glad."

Mr. Teak apologized. "A rich woman," he repeated. "She's been stinting me for twenty-nine years and saving the money—my money!—money that I 'ave earned with the sweat of my brow. She 'as got over three 'undred pounds!"

"'Ow much?" demanded Mr. Chase.

"Three 'undred pounds and more," repeated the other; "and if she had 'ad the sense to put it in a bank it would ha' been over four 'undred by this time. Instead o' that she keeps it hid in the 'Ouse."

"Where?" inquired the greatly interested Mr. Chase.

Mr. Teak shook his head. "That's just what I want to find out," he answered. "She don't know I know it; and she mustn't know, either. That's important."

"How did you find out about it, then?" inquired his friend.

"My wife's sister's husband, Bert Adams, told me. His wife told 'im in strict confidence; and I might 'ave gone to my grave without knowing about it, only she smacked his face for 'im the other night."

"If it's in the house you ought to be able to find it easy enough," said Mr. Chase.

"Yes, it's all very well to talk," retorted Mr. Teak. "My missis never leaves the 'ouse unless I'm with her, except when I'm at work; and if she thought I knew of it she'd take and put it in some bank or somewhere unbeknown to me, and I should be farther off it than ever."

"Haven't you got no idea?" said Mr. Chase.

"Not the leastest bit," said the other. "I never thought for a moment she was saving money. She's always asking me for more, for one thing; but, then women alway do. And look 'ow bad it is for her—saving money like that on the sly. She might grow into a miser, pore thing. For 'er own sake I ought to get hold of it, if it's only to save her from 'erself."

Mr. Chase's face reflected the gravity of his own.

"You're the only man I can trust," continued Mr. Teak, "and I thought if you came as lodger you might be able to find out where it is hid, and get hold of it for me."

"Me steal it, d'ye mean?" demanded the gaping Mr. Chase. "And suppose she got me locked up for it? I should look pretty, shouldn't I?"

"No; you find out where it is hid," said the other; "that's all you need do. I'll find someway of getting hold of it then."

"But if you can't find it, how should I be able to?" inquired Mr. Chase.

"'Cos you'll 'ave opportunities," said the other. "I take her out some time when you're supposed to be out late; you come 'ome, let yourself in with your key, and spot the hiding-place. I get the cash, and give you ten-golden-sovereigns—all to your little self. It only occurred to me after Bert told me about it, that I ain't been in the house alone for years."

He ordered some more beer, and, drawing Mr. Chase to a bench, sat down to a long and steady argument. It shook his faith in human nature to find that his friend estimated the affair as a twenty-pound job, but he was in no position to bargain. They came out smoking twopenny cigars whose strength was remarkable for their age, and before they parted Mr. Chase was pledged to the hilt to do all that he could to save Mrs. Teak from the vice of avarice.

It was a more difficult undertaking than he had supposed. The house, small and compact, seemed to offer few opportunities for the concealment of large sums of money, and after a fortnight's residence he came to the conclusion that the treasure must have been hidden in the garden. The unalloyed pleasure, however, with which Mrs. Teak regarded the efforts of her husband to put under cultivation land that had lain fallow for twenty years convinced both men that they were on a wrong scent. Mr. Teak, who did the digging, was the first to realize it, but his friend, pointing out the suspicions that might be engendered by a sudden cessation of labour, induced him to persevere.

"And try and look as if you liked it," he said, severely. "Why, from the window even the back view of you looks disagreeable."

"I'm fair sick of it," declared Mr. Teak. "Anybody might ha' known she wouldn't have buried it in the garden. She must 'ave been saving for pretty near thirty years, week by week, and she couldn't keep coming out here to hide it. 'Tain't likely."

Mr. Chase pondered. "Let her know, casual like, that I sha'n't be 'ome till late on Saturday," he said, slowly. "Then you come 'ome in the afternoon and take her out. As soon as you're gone I'll pop in and have a thorough good hunt round. Is she fond of animals?"

"I b'lieve so," said the other, staring. "Why?"

"Take 'er to the Zoo," said Mr. Chase, impressively. "Take two-penn'orth o' nuts with you for the monkeys, and some stale buns for—for—for animals as likes 'em. Give 'er a ride on the elephant and a ride on the camel."

"Anything else?" inquired Mr. Teak disagreeably. "Any more ways you can think of for me to spend my money?"

"You do as I tell you," said his friend. "I've got an idea now where it is. If I'm able to show you where to put your finger on three 'undred pounds when you come 'ome it'll be the cheapest outing you have ever 'ad. Won't it?"

Mr. Teak made no reply, but, after spending the evening in deliberation, issued the invitation at the supper-table. His wife's eyes sparkled at first; then the light slowly faded from them and her face fell.

"I can't go," she said, at last. "I've got nothing to go in."

"Rubbish!" said her husband, starting uneasily.

"It's a fact," said Mrs. Teak. "I should like to go, too—it's years since I was at the Zoo. I might make my jacket do; it's my hat I'm thinking about."

Mr. Chase, meeting Mr. Teak's eye, winked an obvious suggestion.

"So, thanking you all the same," continued Mrs. Teak, with amiable cheerfulness, "I'll stay at 'ome."

"'Ow-'ow much are they?" growled her husband, scowling at Mr. Chase.

"All prices," replied his wife.

"Yes, I know," said Mr. Teak, in a grating voice. "You go in to buy a hat at one and eleven-pence; you get talked over and flattered by a man like a barber's block, and you come out with a four-and-six penny one. The only real difference in hats is the price, but women can never see it."

Mrs. Teak smiled faintly, and again expressed her willingness to stay at home. They could spend the afternoon working in the garden, she said. Her husband, with another indignant glance at the right eye of Mr. Chase, which was still enacting the part of a camera-shutter, said that she could have a hat, but asked her to remember when buying it that nothing suited her so well as a plain one.

The remainder of the week passed away slowly; and Mr. Teak, despite his utmost efforts, was unable to glean any information from Mr. Chase as to that gentleman's ideas concerning the hiding-place. At every suggestion Mr. Chase's smile only got broader and more indulgent.

"You leave it to me," he said. "You leave it to me, and when you come home from a happy outing I 'ope to be able to cross your little hand with three 'undred golden quids."

"But why not tell me?" urged Mr. Teak.

"'Cos I want to surprise you," was the reply. "But mind, whatever you do, don't let your wife run away with the idea that I've been mixed up in it at all. Now, if you worry me any more I shall ask you to make it thirty pounds for me instead of twenty."

The two friends parted at the corner of the road on Saturday afternoon, and Mr. Teak, conscious of his friend's impatience, sought to hurry his wife by occasionally calling the wrong time up the stairs. She came down at last, smiling, in a plain hat with three roses, two bows, and a feather.

"I've had the feather for years," she remarked. "This is the fourth hat it has been on—but, then, I've taken care of it."

Mr. Teak grunted, and, opening the door, ushered her into the street. A sense of adventure, and the hope of a profitable afternoon made his spirits rise. He paid a compliment to the hat, and then, to the surprise of both, followed it up with another—a very little one—to his wife.

They took a tram at the end of the street, and for the sake of the air mounted to the top. Mrs. Teak leaned back in her seat with placid enjoyment, and for the first ten minutes amused herself with the life in the streets. Then she turned suddenly to her husband and declared that she had felt a spot of rain.

"'Magination," he said, shortly.

Something cold touched him lightly on the eyelid, a tiny pattering sounded from the seats, and then swish, down came the rain. With an angry exclamation he sprang up and followed his wife below.

"Just our luck," she said, mournfully. "Best thing we can do is to stay in the car and go back with it."

"Nonsense!" said her husband, in a startled' voice; "it'll be over in a minute."

Events proved the contrary. By the time the car reached the terminus it was coming down heavily. Mrs. Teak settled herself squarely in her seat, and patches of blue sky, visible only to the eye of faith and her husband, failed to move her. Even his reckless reference to a cab failed.

"It's no good," she said, tartly. "We can't go about the grounds in a cab, and I'm not going to slop about in the wet to please anybody. We must go another time. It's hard luck, but there's worse things in life."

Mr. Teak, wondering as to the operations of Mr. Chase, agreed dumbly. He stopped the car at the corner of their road, and, holding his head down against the rain, sprinted towards home. Mrs. Teak, anxious for her hat, passed him.

"What on earth's the matter?" she inquired, fumbling in her pocket for the key as her husband executed a clumsy but noisy breakdown on the front step.

"Chill," replied Mr. Teak. "I've got wet."

He resumed his lumberings and, the door being opened, gave vent to his relief at being home again in the dry, in a voice that made the windows rattle. Then with anxious eyes he watched his wife pass upstairs.

"Wonder what excuse old Alf'll make for being in?" he thought.

He stood with one foot on the bottom stair, listening acutely. He heard a door open above, and then a wild, ear-splitting shriek rang through the house. Instinctively he dashed upstairs and, following his wife into their bedroom, stood by her side gaping stupidly at a pair of legs standing on the hearthstone. As he watched they came backwards into the room, the upper part of a body materialized from the chimney, and turning round revealed the soot-stained face of Mr. Alfred Chase. Another wild shriek from Mrs. Teak greeted its appearance.

"Hul-lo!" exclaimed Mr. Teak, groping for the right thing to say. "Hul-lo! What—what are you doing, Alf?"

Mr. Chase blew the soot from his lips. "I—I—I come 'ome unexpected," he stammered.

"But—what are—you doing?" panted Mrs. Teak, in a rising voice.

"I—I was passing your door," said Mr. Chase, "passing your door—to go to my room to—to 'ave a bit of a rinse, when—"

"Yes," said Mrs. Teak.

Mr. Chase gave Mr. Teak a glance the pathos of which even the soot could not conceal. "When I—I heard a pore little bird struggling in your chimbley," he continued, with a sigh of relief. "Being fond of animals, I took the liberty of comin' into your room and saving its life."

Mr. Teak drew a breath, which he endeavoured in vain to render noiseless.

"It got its pore little foot caught in the brickwork," continued the veracious Mr. Chase, tenderly. "I released it, and it flowed—I mean flew—up the chimbley."

With the shamefaced air of a man detected in the performance of a noble action, he passed out of the room. Husband and wife eyed each other.

"That's Alf—that's Alf all over," said Mr. Teak, with enthusiasm. "He's been like it from a child. He's the sort of man that 'ud dive off Waterloo Bridge to save the life of a drownding sparrow."

"He's made an awful mess," said his wife, frowning; "it'll take me the rest of the day to clean up. There's soot everywhere. The rug is quite spoilt."

She took off her hat and jacket and prepared for the fray. Down below Messrs. Teak and Chase, comparing notes, sought, with much warmth, to put the blame on the right shoulders.

"Well, it ain't there," said Mr. Chase, finally. "I've made sure of that. That's something towards it. I shan't 'ave to look there again, thank goodness."

Mr. Teak sniffed. "Got any more ideas?" he queried.

"I have," said the other sternly. "There's plenty of places to search yet. I've only just begun. Get her out as much as you can and I'll 'ave my hands on it afore you can say—"

"Soot?" suggested Mr. Teak, sourly.

"Any more of your nasty snacks and I chuck it up altogether," said Mr. Chase, heatedly. "If I wasn't hard up I'd drop it now."

He went up to his room in dudgeon, and for the next few days Mr. Teak saw but little of him. To, lure Mrs. Teak out was almost as difficult as to persuade a snail to leave its shell, but he succeeded on two or three occasions, and each time she added something to her wardrobe.

The assistant fortune-hunter had been in residence just a month when Mr. Teak, returning home one afternoon, stood in the small passage listening to a suppressed wailing noise proceeding from upstairs. It was so creepy that half-way up he hesitated, and, in a stern but trembling voice, demanded to know what his wife meant by it. A louder wail than before was the only reply, and, summoning up his courage, he pushed open the door of the bedroom and peeped in. His gaze fell on Mrs. Teak, who was sitting on the hearth-rug, rocking to and fro in front of a dismantled fire-place.

"What—what's the matter?" he said, hastily.

Mrs. Teak raised her voice to a pitch that set his teeth on edge. "My money!" she wailed. "It's all gone! All gone!"

"Money?" repeated Mr. Teak, hardly able to contain himself. "What money?"

"All—all my savings!" moaned his wife. "Savings!" said the delighted Mr. Teak. "What savings?"

"Money I have been putting by for our old age," said his wife. "Three hundred and twenty-two pounds. All gone!"

In a fit of sudden generosity Mr. Teak decided then and there that Mr. Chase should have the odd twenty-two pounds.

"You're dreaming!" he said, sternly.

"I wish I was," said his wife, wiping her eyes. "Three hundred and twenty-two pounds in empty mustard-tins. Every ha'penny's gone!"

Mr. Teak's eye fell on the stove. He stepped for ward and examined it. The back was out, and Mrs. Teak, calling his attention to a tunnel at the side, implored him to put his arm in and satisfy himself that it was empty.

"But where could you get all that money from?" he demanded, after a prolonged groping.

"Sa—sa—saved it," sobbed his wife, "for our old age."

"Our old age?" repeated Mr. Teak, in lofty tones. "And suppose I had died first? Or suppose you had died sudden? This is what comes of deceitfulness and keeping things from your husband. Now somebody has stole it."

Mrs. Teak bent her head and sobbed again. "I—I had just been out for —for an hour," she gasped. "When I came back I fou—fou—found the washhouse window smashed, and—"

Sobs choked her utterance. Mr. Teak, lost in admiration of Mr. Chase's cleverness, stood regarding her in silence.

"What—what about the police?" said his wife at last.

"Police!" repeated Mr. Teak, with extraordinary vehemence. "Police! Certainly not. D'ye think I'm going to let it be known all round that I'm the husband of a miser? I'd sooner lose ten times the money."

He stalked solemnly out of the room and downstairs, and, safe in the parlour, gave vent to his feelings in a wild but silent hornpipe. He cannoned against the table at last, and, subsiding into an easy-chair, crammed his handkerchief to his mouth and gave way to suppressed mirth.

In his excitement he forgot all about tea, and the bereaved Mrs. Teak made no attempt to come downstairs to prepare it. With his eye on the clock he waited with what patience he might for the arrival of Mr. Chase. The usual hour for his return came and went. Another hour passed; and another. A horrible idea that Mr. Chase had been robbed gave way to one more horrible still. He paced the room in dismay, until at nine o'clock his wife came down, and in a languid fashion began to set the supper-table.

"Alf's very late," said Mr. Teak, thickly.

"Is he?" said his wife, dully.

"Very late," said Mr. Teak. "I can't think—Ah, there he is!"

He took a deep breath and clenched 'his hands together. By the time Mr. Chase came into the room he was able to greet him with a stealthy wink. Mr. Chase, with a humorous twist of his mouth, winked back.

"We've 'ad a upset," said Mr. Teak, in warning tones.

"Eh?" said the other, as Mrs. Teak threw her apron over her head and sank into a chair. "What about?"

In bated accents, interrupted at times by broken murmurs from his wife, Mr. Teak informed him of the robbery. Mr. Chase, leaning against the doorpost, listened with open mouth and distended eyeballs. Occasional interjections of pity and surprise attested his interest. The tale finished, the gentlemen exchanged a significant wink and sighed in unison.

"And now," said Mr. Teak an hour later, after his wife had retired, "where is it?"

"Ah, that's the question," said Mr. Chase, roguishly. "I wonder where it can be?"

"I—I hope it's in a safe place," said Mr. Teak, anxiously. "Where 'ave you put it?"

"Me?" said Mr. Chase. "Who are you getting at? I ain't put it anywhere. You know that."

"Don't play the giddy goat," said the other, testily. "Where've you hid it? Is it safe?"

Mr. Chase leaned back in his chair and, shaking his head at him, smiled approvingly. "You're a little wonder, that's what you are, Gussie," he remarked. "No wonder your pore wife is took in so easy."

Mr. Teak sprang up in a fury. "Don't play the fool," he said hoarsely. "Where's the money? I want it. Now, where've you put it?"

"Go on," said Mr. Chase, with a chuckle. "Go on. Don't mind me. You ought to be on the stage, Gussie, that's where you ought to be."

"I'm not joking," said Mr. Teak, in a trembling voice, "and I don't want you to joke with me. If you think you are going off with my money, you're mistook. If you don't tell me in two minutes where it is, I shall give you in charge for theft."

"Oh" said Mr. Chase. He took a deep breath. "Oh, really!" he said. "I wouldn't 'ave thought it of you, Gussie. I wouldn't 'ave thought you'd have played it so low down. I'm surprised at you."

"You thought wrong, then," said the other.

"Trying to do me out o' my twenty pounds, that's what you are," said Mr. Chase, knitting his brows. "But it won't do, my boy. I wasn't born yesterday. Hand it over, afore I lose my temper. Twenty pounds I want of you, and I don't leave this room till I get it."

Speechless with fury, Mr. Teak struck at him. The next moment the supper-table was overturned with a crash, and Mr. Chase, with his friend in his powerful grasp, was doing his best, as he expressed it, to shake the life out of him. A faint scream sounded from above, steps pattered on the stairs, and Mrs. Teak, with a red shawl round her shoulders, burst 'hurriedly into the room. Mr. Chase released Mr. Teak, opened his mouth to speak, and then, thinking better of it, dashed into the passage, took his hat from the peg, and, slamming the front door with extraordinary violence, departed.

He sent round for his clothes next day, but he did not see Mr. Teak until a month afterwards. His fists clenched and his mouth hardened, but Mr. Teak, with a pathetic smile, held out his hand, and Mr. Chase, after a moment's hesitation, took it. Mr. Teak, still holding his friend's hand, piloted him to a neighbouring hostelry.

"It was my mistake, Alf," he said, shaking his head, "but it wasn't my fault. It's a mistake anybody might ha' made."

"Have you found out who took it?" inquired Mr. Chase, regarding him suspiciously.

Mr. Teak gulped and nodded. "I met Bert Adams yesterday," he said, slowly. "It took three pints afore he told me, but I got it out of 'im at last. My missis took it herself."

Mr. Chase put his mug down with a bang. "What?" he gasped.

"The day after she found you with your head up the chimbley," added Mr. Teak, mournfully. "She's shoved it away in some bank now, and I shall never see a ha'penny of it. If you was a married man, Alf, you'd understand it better. You wouldn't be surprised at anything."

FALSE COLOURS

Of course, there is a deal of bullying done at sea at times," said the night-watchman, thoughtfully. 'The men call it bullying an' the officers call it discipline, but it's the same thing under another name. Still, it's fair in a way. It gets passed on from one to another. Everybody aboard a'most has got somebody to bully, except, perhaps, the boy; he 'as the worst of it, unless he can manage to get the ship's cat by itself occasionally.

"I don't think sailor-men mind being bullied. I never 'eard of its putting one off 'is feed yet, and that's the main thing, arter all's said and done.

"Fust officers are often worse than skippers. In the fust place, they know they ain't skippers, an' that alone is enough to put 'em in a bad temper, especially if they've 'ad their certifikit a good many years and can't get a vacancy.

"I remember, a good many years ago now, I was lying at Calcutta one time in the Peewit, as fine a barque as you'd wish to see, an' we 'ad a fust mate there as was a disgrace to 'is sects. A nasty, bullying, violent man, who used to call the hands names as they didn't know the meanings of and what was no use looking in the dictionary for.

"There was one chap aboard, Bill Cousins, as he used to make a partikler mark of. Bill 'ad the misfortin to 'ave red 'air, and the way the mate used to throw that in 'is face was disgraceful. Fortunately for us all, the skipper was a very decent sort of man, so that the mate was only at 'is worst when he wasn't by.

"We was sitting in the fo'c's'le at tea one arter-noon, when Bill Cousins came down, an' we see at once 'e'd 'ad a turn with the mate. He sat all by hisself for some time simmering, an' then he broke out. 'One o' these days I'll swing for 'im; mark my words.'

"'Don't be a fool, Bill,' ses Joe Smith.

"'If I could on'y mark 'im,' ses Bill, catching his breath. 'Just mark 'im fair an' square. If I could on'y 'ave 'im alone for ten minutes, with nobody standing by to see fair play. But, o' course, if I 'it 'im it's mutiny.'

"'You couldn't do it if it wasn't, Bill,' ses Joe Smith again.

"'He walks about the town as though the place belongs to 'im,' said Ted Hill. 'Most of us is satisfied to shove the niggers out o' the way, but he ups fist and 'its 'em if they comes within a yard of 'im.'

"'Why don't they 'it 'im back?' ses Bill. 'I would if I was them.'

"Joe Smith grunted. 'Well, why don't you?' he asked.

"'Cos I ain't a nigger,' ses Bill.

"'Well, but you might be,' ses Joe, very softly. 'Black your face an' 'ands an' legs, and dress up in them cotton things, and go ashore and get in 'is way.'

"'If you will, I will, Bill,' ses a chap called Bob Pullin.

"Well, they talked it over and over, and at last Joe, who seemed to take a great interest in it, went ashore and got the duds for 'em. They was a tight fit for Bill, Hindoos not being as wide as they might be, but Joe said if 'e didn't bend about he'd be all right, and Pullin, who was a smaller man, said his was fust class.

"After they were dressed, the next question was wot to use to colour them with; coal was too scratchy, an' ink Bill didn't like. Then Ted Hill burnt a cork and started on Bill's nose with it afore it was cool, an' Bill didn't like that.

"'Look 'ere,' ses the carpenter, 'nothin' seems to please you, Bill—it's my opinion you're backing out of it.'

"'You're a liar,' ses Bill.

"'Well, I've got some stuff in a can as might be boiled-down Hindoo for all you could tell to the difference,' ses the carpenter; 'and if you'll keep that ugly mouth of yours shut, I'll paint you myself.'

"Well, Bill was a bit flattered, the carpenter being a very superior sort of a man, and quite an artist in 'is way, an' Bill sat down an' let 'im do 'im with some stuff out of a can that made 'im look like a Hindoo what 'ad been polished. Then Bob Pullin was done too, an' when they'd got their turbins on, the change in their appearance was wonderful.

"'Feels a bit stiff,' ses Bill, working 'is mouth.

"'That ll wear off,' ses the carpenter; 'it wouldn't be you if you didn't 'ave a grumble, Bill.'

"'And mind and don't spare 'im, Bill,' ses Joe. 'There's two of you, an' if you only do wot's expected of you, the mate ought to 'ave a easy time abed this v'y'ge.'

"'Let the mate start fust,' ses Ted Hill. 'He's sure to start on you if you only get in 'is way. Lord, I'd like to see his face when you start on 'im.

"Well, the two of 'em went ashore arter dark with the best wishes o' all on board, an' the rest of us sat down in the fo'c's'le spekerlating as to what sort o' time the mate was goin' to 'ave. He went ashore all right, because Ted Hill see 'im go, an' he noticed with partikler pleasure as 'ow he was dressed very careful.

"It must ha' been near eleven o'clock. I was sitting with Smith on the port side o' the galley, when we heard a 'ubbub approaching the ship. It was the mate just coming aboard. He was without 'is 'at; 'is necktie was twisted round 'is ear, and 'is shirt and 'is collar was all torn to shreds. The second and third officers ran up to him to see what was the matter, and while he was telling them, up comes the skipper.

"'You don't mean to tell me, Mr. Fingall,' ses the skipper, in surprise, 'that you've been knocked about like that by them mild and meek Hindoos?'

"'Hindoos, sir?' roared the mate. 'Certainly not, sir. I've been assaulted like this by five German sailor-men. And I licked 'em all.'

"'I'm glad to hear that,' ses the skipper; and the second and third pats the mate on the back, just like you pat a dog you don't know.

"'Big fellows they was,' ses he, 'an' they give me some trouble. Look at my eye!'

"The second officer struck a match and looked at it, and it cert'n'y was a beauty.

"'I hope you reported this at the police station?' ses the skipper.

"'No, sir,' ses the mate, holding up 'is 'ead. 'I don't want no p'lice to protect me. Five's a large number, but I drove 'em off, and I don't think they'll meddle with any British fust officers again.'

"'You'd better turn in,' ses the second, leading him off by the arm.

"The mate limped off with him, and as soon as the coast was clear we put our 'eads together and tried to make out how it was that Bill Cousins and Bob 'ad changed themselves into five German sailor-men.

"'It's the mate's pride,' ses the carpenter. 'He didn't like being knocked about by Hindoos.'

"We thought it was that, but we had to wait nearly another hour afore the two came aboard, to make sure. There was a difference in the way they came aboard, too, from that of the mate. They didn't make no noise, and the fust thing we knew of their coming aboard was seeing a bare, black foot waving feebly at the top of the fo'c's'le ladder feelin' for the step.

"That was Bob. He came down without a word, and then we see 'e was holding another black foot and guiding it to where it should go. That was Bill, an' of all the 'orrid, limp-looking blacks that you ever see, Bill was the worst when he got below. He just sat on a locker all of a heap and held 'is 'ead, which was swollen up, in 'is hands. Bob went and sat beside 'im, and there they sat, for all the world like two wax figgers instead o' human beings.

"'Well, you done it, Bill,' ses Joe, after waiting a long time for them to speak. 'Tell us all about it.'

"'Nothin' to tell,' ses Bill, very surly. 'We knocked 'im about.'

"'And he knocked us about,' ses Bob, with a groan. 'I'm sore all over, and as for my feet—'

"'Wot's the matter with them?' ses Joe.

"'Trod on,' ses Bob, very short. 'If my bare feet was trod on once they was a dozen times. I've never 'ad such a doing in all my life. He fought like a devil. I thought he'd ha' murdered Bill.'

"'I wish 'e 'ad,' ses Bill, with a groan; 'my face is bruised and cut about cruel. I can't bear to touch it.'

"'Do you mean to say the two of you couldn't settle 'im?' ses Joe, staring.

"'I mean to say we got a hiding,' ses Bill. 'We got close to him fust start off and got our feet trod on. Arter that it was like fighting a windmill, with sledge-hammers for sails.'

"He gave a groan and turned over in his bunk, and when we asked him some more about it, he swore at us. They both seemed quite done up, and at last they dropped off to sleep just as they was, without even stopping to wash the black off or to undress themselves.

"I was awoke rather early in the morning by the sounds of somebody talking to themselves, and a little splashing of water. It seemed to go on a long while, and at last I leaned out of my bunk and see Bill bencing over a bucket and washing himself and using bad langwidge.

"'Wot's the matter, Bill?' ses Joe, yawning and sitting up in bed.

"'My skin's that tender, I can hardly touch it,' ses Bill, bending down and rinsing 'is face. 'Is it all orf?'

"'Orf?' ses Joe; 'no, o' course it ain't. Why don't you use some soap?'

"'Soap,' answers Bill, mad-like; 'why, I've used more soap than I've used for six months in the ordinary way.'

"That's ro good,' ses Joe; 'give yourself a good wash.'

"Bill put down the soap then very careful, and went over to 'im and told him all the dreadful things he'd do to him when he got strong agin, and then Bob Pullin got out of his bunk an' 'ad a try on his face. Him an' Bill kept washing and then taking each other to the light and trying to believe it was coming off until they got sick of it, and then Bill, 'e up with his foot and capsized the bucket, and walked up and down the fo'c's'le raving.

"'Well, the carpenter put it on,' ses a voice, 'make 'im take it orf.'

"You wouldn't believe the job we 'ad to wake that man up. He wasn't fairly woke till he was hauled out of 'is bunk an' set down opposite them two pore black fellers an' told to make 'em white again.

"'I don't believe as there's anything will touch it,' he says, at last. 'I forgot all about that.'

"'Do you mean to say,' bawls Bill, 'that we've got to be black all the rest of our life?'

"'Cert'nly not,' ses the carpenter, indignantly, 'it'll wear off in time; shaving every morning 'll 'elp it, I should say.'

"'I'll get my razor now,' ses Bill, in a awful voice; 'don't let 'im go, Bob. I'll 'ack 'is head orf.'

"He actually went off an' got his razor, but, o' course, we jumped out o' our bunks and got between 'em and told him plainly that it was not to be, and then we set 'em down and tried everything we could think of, from butter and linseed oil to cold tea-leaves used as a poultice, and all it did was to make 'em shinier an' shinier.

"'It's no good, I tell you,' ses the carpenter, 'it's the most lasting black I know. If I told you how much that stuf is a can, you wouldn't believe me.'

"'Well, you're in it,' ses Bill, his voice all of a tremble; 'you done it so as we could knock the mate about. Whatever's done to us'll be done to you too.'

"'I don't think turps'll touch it,' ses the carpenter, getting up, 'but we'll 'ave a try.'

"He went and fetched the can and poured some out on a bit o' rag and told Bill to dab his face with it. Bill give a dab, and the next moment he rushed over with a scream and buried his head in a shirt what Simmons was wearing at the time and began to wipe his face with it. Then he left the flustered Simmons an' shoved another chap away from the bucket and buried his face in it and kicked and carried on like a madman. Then 'e jumped into his bunk again and buried 'is face in the clothes and rocked hisself and moaned as if he was dying.

"'Don't you use it, Bob,' he ses, at last

"''Tain't likely,' ses Bob. 'It's a good thing you tried it fust, Bill.'

"''Ave they tried holy-stone?' ses a voice from a bunk.

"'No, they ain't,' ses Bob, snappishly, 'and, what's more, they ain't goin' to.'

"Both o' their tempers was so bad that we let the subject drop while we was at breakfast. The orkard persition of affairs could no longer be disregarded. Fust one chap threw out a 'int and then another, gradually getting a little stronger and stronger, until Bill turned round in a uncomfortable way and requested of us to leave off talking with our mouths full and speak up like Englishmen wot we meant.

"'You see, it's this way, Bill,' ses Joe, soft-like. 'As soon as the mate sees you there'll be trouble for all of us.'

"'For all of us,' repeats Bill, nodding.

"'Whereas,' ses Joe, looking round for support, 'if we gets up a little collection for you and you should find it convenient to desart.'

"''Ear, 'ear,' ses a lot o' voices. 'Bravo, Joe.'

"'Oh, desart is it?' ses Bill; 'an' where are we goin' to desart to?'

"'Well, that we leave to you,' ses Joe; 'there's many a ship short-'anded as would be glad to pick up sich a couple of prime sailor-men as you an' Bob.'

"'Ah, an' wot about our black faces?' ses Bill, still in the same sneering, ungrateful sort o' voice.

"'That can be got over,' ses Joe.

"'Ow?' ses Bill and Bob together.

"'Ship as nigger cooks,' ses Joe, slapping his knee and looking round triumphant.

"It's no good trying to do some people a kindness. Joe was perfectly sincere, and nobody could say but wot it wasn't a good idea, but o' course Mr. Bill Cousins must consider hisself insulted, and I can only suppose that the trouble he'd gone through 'ad affected his brain. Likewise Bob Pullin's. Anyway, that's the only excuse I can make for 'em. To cut a long story short, nobody 'ad any more breakfast, and no time to do anything until them two men was scrouged up in a corner an' 'eld there unable to move.

"'I'd never 'ave done 'em,' ses the carpenter, arter it was all over, 'if I'd know they was goin' to carry on like this. They wanted to be done.'

"The mate'll half murder 'em,' ses Ted Hill.

"'He'll 'ave 'em sent to gaol, that's wot he'll do,' ses Smith. 'It's a serious matter to go ashore and commit assault and battery on the mate.'

"'You're all in it,' ses the voice o' Bill from the floor. 'I'm going to make a clean breast of it. Joe Smith put us up to it, the carpenter blacked us, and the others encouraged us.'

"'Joe got the clothes for us,' ses Bob. 'I know the place he got 'em from, too.'

"The ingratitude o' these two men was sich that at first we decided to have no more to do with them, but better feelings prevailed, and we held a sort o' meeting to consider what was best to be done. An' everything that was suggested one o' them two voices from the floor found fault with and wouldn't 'ave, and at last we 'ad to go up on deck with nothing decided upon, except to swear 'ard and fast as we knew nothing about it.

"The only advice we can give you,' ses Joe, looking back at 'em, 'is to stay down 'ere as long as you can.'

"A'most the fust person we see on deck was the mate, an' a pretty sight he was. He'd got a bandage round 'is left eye, and a black ring round the other. His nose was swelled and his lip cut, but the other officers were making sich a fuss over 'im, that I think he rather gloried in it than otherwise.

"'Where's them other two 'ands?' he ses, by and by, glaring out of 'is black eye.

"'Down below, sir, I b'lieve,' ses the carpenter, all of a tremble.

"'Go an' send 'em up,' ses the mate to Smith.

"'Yessir,' ses Joe, without moving.

"'Well, go on then,' roars the mate.

"'They ain't over and above well, sir, this morning,' ses Joe.

"'Send 'em up, confound you,' ses the mate, limping towards 'im.

"Well, Joe give 'is shoulders a 'elpless sort o' shrug and walked forward and bawled down the fo'c's'le.

"'They're coming, sir,' he ses, walking bade to the mate just as the skipper came out of 'is cabin.

"We all went on with our work as 'ard as we knew 'ow. The skipper was talking to the mate about 'is injuries, and saying unkind things about Germans, when he give a sort of a shout and staggered back staring. We just looked round, and there was them two blackamoors coming slowly towards us.

"'Good heavens, Mr. Fingall,' ses the old man. 'What's this?'

"I never see sich a look on any man's face as I saw on the mate's then. Three times 'e opened 'is mouth to speak, and shut it agin without saying anything. The veins on 'is forehead swelled up tremendous and 'is cheeks was all blown out purple.

"That's Bill Cousins's hair,' ses the skipper to himself. 'It's Bill Cousins's hair. It's Bill Cous—'

"Bob walked up to him, with Bill lagging a little way behind, and then he stops just in front of 'im and fetches up a sort o' little smile.

"'Don't you make those faces at me, sir?' roars the skipper. 'What do you mean by it? What have you been doing to yourselves?'

"'Nothin', sir,' ses Bill, 'umbly; 'it was done to us.'

"The carpenter, who was just going to cooper up a cask which 'ad started a bit, shook like a leaf, and gave Bill a look that would ha' melted a stone.

"'Who did it?' ses the skipper.

"'We've been the wictims of a cruel outrage, sir,' ses Bill, doing all 'e could to avoid the mate's eye, which wouldn't be avoided.

"'So I should think,' ses the skipper. 'You've been knocked about, too.'

"'Yessir,' ses Bill, very respectful; 'me and Bob was ashore last night, sir, just for a quiet look round, when we was set on to by five furriners.'

"'What?' ses the skipper; and I won't repeat what the mate said.

"'We fought 'em as long as we could, sir,' ses Bill, 'then we was both knocked senseless, and when we came to ourselves we was messed up like this 'ere.'

"What sort o' men were they?' asked the skipper, getting excited.

"'Sailor-men, sir,' ses Bob, putting in his spoke. 'Dutchies or Germans, or something o' that sort.'

"'Was there one tall man, with a fair beard,' ses the skipper, getting more and more excited.

"'Yessir,' ses Bill, in a surprised sort o' voice.

"'Same gang,' ses the skipper. 'Same gang as knocked Mr. Fingall about, you may depend upon it. Mr. Fingall, it's a mercy for you you didn't get your face blacked too.'

"I thought the mate would ha' burst. I can't understand how any man could swell as he swelled without bursting.

"'I don't believe a word of it,' he ses, at last.

"'Why not?' ses the skipper, sharply.

"'Well, I don't,' ses the mate, his voice trembling with passion. 'I 'ave my reasons.'

"'I s'pose you don't think these two poor fellows went and blacked themselves for fun, do you?' ses the skipper.

"The mate couldn't answer.

"'And then went and knocked themselves about for more fun?' ses the skipper, very sarcastic.

"The mate didn't answer. He looked round helpless like, and see the third officer swopping glances with the second, and all the men looking sly and amused, and I think if ever a man saw 'e was done 'e did at that moment.

"He turned away and went below, and the skipper arter reading us all a little lecture on getting into fights without reason, sent the two chaps below agin and told 'em to turn in and rest. He was so good to 'em all the way 'ome, and took sich a interest in seeing 'em change from black to brown and from light brown to spotted lemon, that the mate daren't do nothing to them, but gave us their share of what he owed them, as well as an extra dose of our own."

FAMILY CARES

Mr. Jernshaw, who was taking the opportunity of a lull in business to weigh out pound packets of sugar, knocked his hands together and stood waiting for the order of the tall bronzed man who had just entered the shop—a well-built man of about forty—who was regarding him with blue eyes set in quizzical wrinkles.

"What, Harry!" exclaimed Mr. Jernshaw, in response to the wrinkles. "Harry Barrett!"

"That's me," said the other, extending his hand. "The rolling stone come home covered with moss."

Mr. Jernshaw, somewhat excited, shook hands, and led the way into the little parlour behind the shop.

"Fifteen years," said Mr. Barrett, sinking into a chair, "and the old place hasn't altered a bit."

"Smithson told me he had let that house in Webb Street to a Barrett," said the grocer, regarding him, "but I never thought of you. I suppose you've done well, then?"

Mr. Barrett nodded. "Can't grumble," he said modestly. "I've got enough to live on. Melbourne's all right, but I thought I'd come home for the evening of my life."

"Evening!" repeated his friend. "Forty-three," said Mr. Barrett, gravely. "I'm getting on."

"You haven't changed much," said the grocer, passing his hand through his spare grey whiskers. "Wait till you have a wife and seven youngsters. Why, boots alone—"

Mr. Barrett uttered a groan intended for sympathy. "Perhaps you could help me with the furnishing," he said, slowly. "I've never had a place of my own before, and I don't know much about it."

"Anything I can do," said his friend. "Better not get much yet; you might marry, and my taste mightn't be hers."

Mr. Barrett laughed. "I'm not marrying," he said, with conviction.

"Seen anything of Miss Prentice yet?" inquired Mr. Jernshaw.

"No," said the other, with a slight flush. "Why?"

"She's still single," said the grocer.

"What of it?" demanded Mr. Barrett, with warmth. "What of it?"

"Nothing," said Mr. Jernshaw, slowly. "Nothing; only I—"

"Well?" said the other, as he paused.

"I—there was an idea that you went to Australia to—to better your condition," murmured the grocer. "That—that you were not in a position to marry—that—"

"Boy and girl nonsense," said Mr. Barrett, sharply. "Why, it's fifteen years ago. I don't suppose I should know her if I saw her. Is her mother alive?"

"Rather!" said Mr. Jernshaw, with emphasis. "Louisa is something like what her mother was when you went away."

Mr. Barrett shivered.

"But you'll see for yourself," continued the other. "You'll have to go and see them. They'll wonder you haven't been before."

"Let 'em wonder," said the embarrassed Mr. Barrett. "I shall go and see all my old friends in their turn; casual-like. You might let 'em hear that I've been to see you before seeing them, and then, if they're thinking any nonsense, it'll be a hint. I'm stopping in town while the house is being decorated; next time I come down I'll call and see somebody else."

"That'll be another hint," assented Mr. Jernshaw. "Not that hints are much good to Mrs. Prentice."

"We'll see," said Mr. Barrett.

In accordance with his plan his return to his native town was heralded by a few short visits at respectable intervals. A sort of human butterfly, he streaked rapidly across one or two streets, alighted for half an hour to resume an old friendship, and then disappeared again. Having given at least half-a-dozen hints of this kind, he made a final return to Ramsbury and entered into occupation of his new house.

"It does you credit, Jernshaw," he said, gratefully. "I should have made a rare mess of it without your help."

"It looks very nice," admitted his friend. "Too nice."

"That's all nonsense," said the owner, irritably.

"All right," said Mr. Jernshaw. "I don't know the sex, then, that's all. If you think that you're going to keep a nice house like this all to yourself, you're mistaken. It's a home; and where there's a home a woman comes in, somehow."

Mr. Barrett grunted his disbelief.

"I give you four days," said Mr. Jernshaw.

As a matter of fact, Mrs. Prentice and her daughter came on the fifth. Mr. Barrett, who was in an easy-chair, wooing slumber with a handkerchief over his head, heard their voices at the front door and the cordial invitation of his housekeeper. They entered the room as he sat hastily smoothing his rumpled hair.

"Good afternoon," he said, shaking hands.

Mrs. Prentice returned the greeting in a level voice, and, accepting a chair, gazed around the room.

"Nice weather," said Mr. Barrett.

"Very," said Mrs. Prentice.

"It's—it's quite a pleasure to see you again," said Mr. Barrett.

"We thought we should have seen you before," said Mrs. Prentice, "but I told Louisa that no doubt you were busy, and wanted to surprise her. I like the carpet; don't you, Louisa?"

Miss Prentice said she did.

"The room is nice and airy," said Mrs. Prentice, "but it's a pity you didn't come to me before deciding. I could have told you of a better house for the same money."

"I'm very well satisfied with this," said Mr. Barrett. "It's all I want."

"It's well enough," conceded Mrs. Prentice, amiably. "And how have you been all these years?"

Mr. Barrett, with some haste, replied that his health and spirits had been excellent.

"You look well," said Mrs. Prentice. "Neither of you seem to have changed much," she added, looking from him to her daughter. "And I think you did quite well not to write. I think it was much the best."

Mr. Barrett sought for a question: a natural, artless question, that would neutralize the hideous suggestion conveyed by this remark, but it eluded him. He sat and gazed in growing fear at Mrs. Prentice.

"I—I couldn't write," he said at last, in desperation; "my wife—"

"Your what?" exclaimed Mrs. Prentice, loudly.

"Wife," said Mr. Barrett, suddenly calm now that he had taken the plunge. "She wouldn't have liked it."

Mrs. Prentice tried to control her voice. I never heard you were married!" she gasped. "Why isn't she here?"

"We couldn't agree," said the veracious Mr. Barrett. "She was very difficult; so I left the children with her and—"

"Chil—" said Mrs. Prentice, and paused, unable to complete the word.

"Five," said Mr. Barrett, in tones of resignation. "It was rather a wrench, parting with them, especially the baby. He got his first tooth the day I left."

The information fell on deaf ears. Mrs. Prentice, for once in her life thoroughly at a loss, sat trying to collect her scattered faculties. She had come out prepared for a hard job, but not an impossible one. All things considered, she took her defeat with admirable composure.

"I have no doubt it is much the best thing for the children to remain with their mother," she said, rising.

"Much the best," agreed Mr. Barrett. "Whatever she is like," continued the old lady. "Are you ready, Louisa?"

Mr. Barrett followed them to the door, and then, returning to the room, watched, with glad eyes, their progress up the street.

"Wonder whether she'll keep it to herself?" he muttered.

His doubts were set at rest next day. All Ramsbury knew by then of his matrimonial complications, and seemed anxious to talk about them; complications which tended to increase until Mr. Barrett wrote out a list of his children's names and ages and learnt it off by heart.

Relieved of the attentions of the Prentice family, he walked the streets a free man; and it was counted to him for righteousness that he never said a hard word about his wife. She had her faults, he said, but they were many thousand miles away, and he preferred to forget them. And he added, with some truth, that he owed her a good deal.

For a few months he had no reason to alter his opinion. Thanks to his presence of mind, the Prentice family had no terrors for him. Heart-whole and fancy free, he led the easy life of a man of leisure, a condition of things suddenly upset by the arrival of Miss Grace Lindsay to take up a post at the elementary school. Mr. Barrett succumbed almost at once, and, after a few encounters in the street and meetings at mutual friends', went to unbosom him-self to Mr. Jernshaw.

"What has she got to do with you?" demanded that gentleman.

"I—I'm rather struck with her," said Mr. Barrett.

"Struck with her?" repeated his friend, sharply. "I'm surprised at you. You've no business to think of such things."

"Why not?" demanded Mr. Barrett, in tones that were sharper still.

"Why not?" repeated the other. "Have you forgotten your wife and children?"

Mr. Barrett, who, to do him justice, had forgotten, fell back in his chair and sat gazing at him, open-mouthed.

"You're in a false position—in a way," said Mr. Jernshaw, sternly.

"False is no name for it," said Mr. Barrett, huskily. "What am I to do?"

"Do?" repeated the other, staring at him. "Nothing! Unless, perhaps, you send for your wife and children. I suppose, in any case, you would have to have the little ones if anything happened to her?"

Mr. Barrett grinned ruefully.

"Think it over," said Mr. Jernshaw. "I will," said the other, heartily.

He walked home deep in thought. He was a kindly man, and he spent some time thinking out the easiest death for Mrs. Barrett. He decided at last upon heart-disease, and a fort-night later all Ramsbury knew of the letter from Australia conveying the mournful intelligence. It was generally agreed that the mourning and the general behaviour of the widower left nothing to be desired.

"She's at peace at last," he said, solemnly, to Jernshaw.

"I believe you killed her," said his friend. Mr. Barrett started violently.

"I mean your leaving broke her heart," explained the other.

Mr. Barrett breathed easily again.

"It's your duty to look after the children," said Jernshaw, firmly. "And I'm not the only one that thinks so."

"They are with their grandfather and grand-mother," said Mr. Barrett.

Mr. Jernshaw sniffed.

"And four uncles and five aunts," added Mr. Barrett, triumphantly.

"Think how they would brighten up your house," said Mr. Jernshaw.

His friend shook his head. "It wouldn't be fair to their grandmother," he said, decidedly. "Besides, Australia wants population."

He found to his annoyance that Mr. Jernshaw's statement that he was not alone in his views was correct. Public opinion seemed to expect the arrival of the children, and one citizen even went so far as to recommend a girl he knew, as nurse.

Ramsbury understood at last that his decision was final, and, observing his attentions to the new schoolmistress, flattered itself that it had discovered the reason. It is possible that Miss Lindsay shared their views, but if so she made no sign, and on the many occasions on which she met Mr. Barrett on her way to and from school greeted him with frank cordiality. Even when he referred to his loneliness, which he did frequently, she made no comment.

He went into half-mourning at the end of two months, and a month later bore no outward signs of his loss. Added to that his step was springy and his manner youthful. Miss Lindsay was twenty-eight, and he persuaded himself that, sexes considered, there was no disparity worth mentioning.

He was only restrained from proposing by a question of etiquette. Even a shilling book on the science failed to state the interval that should elapse between the death of one wife and the negotiations for another. It preferred instead to give minute instructions with regard to the eating of asparagus. In this dilemma he consulted Jernshaw.

"Don't know, I'm sure," said that gentle-man; "besides, it doesn't matter."

"Doesn't matter?" repeated Mr. Barrett. "Why not?"

"Because I think Tillett is paying her attentions," was the reply. "He's ten years younger than you are, and a bachelor. A girl would naturally prefer him to a middle-aged widower with five children."

"In Australia," the other reminded him.

"Man for man, bachelor for bachelor," said Mr. Jernshaw, regarding him, "she might prefer you; as things are—"

"I shall ask her," said Mr. Barrett, doggedly. "I was going to wait a bit longer, but if there's any chance of her wrecking her prospects for life by marrying that tailor's dummy it's my duty to risk it—for her sake. I've seen him talking to her twice myself, but I never thought he'd dream of such a thing."

Apprehension and indignation kept him awake half the night, but when he arose next morning it was with the firm resolve to put his fortune to the test that day. At four o'clock he changed his neck-tie for the third time, and at ten past sallied out in the direction of the school. He met Miss Lindsay just coming out, and, after a well-deserved compliment to the weather, turned and walked with her.

"I was hoping to meet you," he said, slowly.

"Yes?" said the girl.

"I—I have been feeling rather lonely to-day," he continued.

"You often do," said Miss Lindsay, guardedly.

"It gets worse and worse," said Mr. Barrett, sadly.

"I think I know what is the matter with you," said the girl, in a soft voice; "you have got nothing to do all day, and you live alone, except for your housekeeper."

Mr. Barrett assented with some eagerness, and stole a hopeful glance at her.

"You—you miss something," continued Miss. Lindsay, in a faltering voice.

"I do," said Mr. Barrett, with ardour.

"You miss"—the girl made an effort—"you miss the footsteps and voices of your little children."

Mr. Barrett stopped suddenly in the street, and then, with a jerk, went blindly on.

"I've never spoken of it before because it's your business, not mine," continued the girl. I wouldn't have spoken now, but when you referred to your loneliness I thought perhaps you didn't realize the cause of it."

Mr. Barrett walked on in silent misery.

"Poor little motherless things!" said Miss Lindsay, softly. "Motherless and—fatherless."

"Better for them," said Mr. Barrett, finding his voice at last.

"It almost looks like it," said Miss Lindsay, with a sigh.

Mr. Barrett tried to think clearly, but the circumstances were hardly favourable. "Suppose," he said, speaking very slowly, "suppose I wanted to get married?"

Miss Lindsay started. "What, again?" she said, with an air of surprise.

"How could I ask a girl to come and take over five children?"

"No woman that was worth having would let little children be sacrificed for her sake," said Miss Lindsay, decidedly.

"Do you think anybody would marry me with five children?" demanded Mr. Barrett.

"She might," said the girl, edging away from him a little. "It depends on the woman."

"Would—you, for instance?" said Mr. Barrett, desperately.

Miss Lindsay shrank still farther away. "I don't know; it would depend upon circumstances," she murmured.

"I will write and send for them," said Mr. Barrett, significantly.

Miss Lindsay made no reply. They had arrived at her gate by this time, and, with a hurried handshake, she disappeared indoors.

Mr. Barrett, somewhat troubled in mind, went home to tea.

He resolved, after a little natural hesitation, to drown the children, and reproached himself bitterly for not having disposed of them at the same time as their mother. Now he would have to go through another period of mourning and the consequent delay in pressing his suit. Moreover, he would have to allow a decent interval between his conversation with Miss Lindsay and their untimely end.

The news of the catastrophe arrived two or three days before the return of the girl from her summer holidays. She learnt it in the first half-hour from her landlady, and sat in a dazed condition listening to a description of the grief-stricken father and the sympathy extended to him by his fellow-citizens. It appeared that nothing had passed his lips for two days.

"Shocking!" said Miss Lindsay, briefly. "Shocking !"

An instinctive feeling that the right and proper thing to do was to nurse his grief in solitude kept Mr. Barrett out of her way for nearly a week. When she did meet him she received a limp handshake and a greeting in a voice from which all hope seemed to have departed.

"I am very sorry," she said, with a sort of measured gentleness.

Mr. Barrett, in his hushed voice, thanked her.

"I am all alone now," he said, pathetically. "There is nobody now to care whether I live or die."

Miss Lindsay did not contradict him.

"How did it happen?" she inquired, after they had gone some distance in silence.

"They were out in a sailing-boat," said Mr. Barrett; "the boat capsized in a puff of wind, and they were all drowned."

"Who was in charge of them?" inquired the girl, after a decent interval.

"Boatman," replied the other.

"How did you hear?"

"I had a letter from one of my sisters-in-law, Charlotte," said Mr. Barrett. "A most affecting letter. Poor Charlotte was like a second mother to them. She'll never be the same woman again. Never!"

"I should like to see the letter," said Miss Lindsay, musingly.

Mr. Barrett suppressed a start. "I should like to show it to you," he said, "but I'm afraid I have destroyed it. It made me shudder every time I looked at it."

"It's a pity," said the girl, dryly. "I should have liked to see it. I've got my own idea about the matter. Are you sure she was very fond of them?"

"She lived only for them," said Mr. Barrett, in a rapt voice.

"Exactly. I don't believe they are drowned at all," said Miss Lindsay, suddenly. "I believe you have had all this terrible anguish for nothing. It's too cruel."

Mr. Barrett stared at her in anxious amazement.

"I see it all now," continued the girl. "Their Aunt Charlotte was devoted to them. She always had the fear that some day you would return and claim them, and to prevent that she invented the story of their death."

"Charlotte is the most truthful woman that ever breathed," said the distressed Mr. Barrett.

Miss Lindsay shook her head. "You are like all other honourable, truthful people," she said, looking at him gravely. "You can't imagine anybody else telling a falsehood. I don't believe you could tell one if you tried."

Mr. Barrett gazed about him with the despairing look of a drowning mariner.

"I'm certain I'm right," continued the girl. "I can see Charlotte exulting in her wickedness. Why!"

"What's the matter?" inquired Mr. Barrett, greatly worried.

"I've just thought of it," said Miss Lindsay. "She's told you that your children are drowned, and she has probably told them you are dead. A woman like that would stick at nothing to gain her ends."

"You don't know Charlotte," said Mr. Barrett, feebly.

"I think do," was the reply. "However, we'll make sure. I suppose you've got friends in Melbourne?"

"A few,' said Mr. Barrett, guardedly.

"Come down to the post-office and cable to one of them."

Mr. Barrett hesitated. "I'll write," he said, slowly. "It's an awkward thing to cable; and there's no hurry. I'll write to Jack Adams, I think."

"It's no good writing," said Miss Lindsay, firmly. "You ought to know that."

"Why not?" demanded the other.

"Because, you foolish man," said the girl, calmly, "before your letter got there, there would be one from Melbourne saying that he had been choked by a fish-bone, or died of measles, or something of that sort."

Mr. Barrett, hardly able to believe his ears, stopped short and looked at her. The girl's eyes were moist with mirth and her lips trembling. He put out his hand and took her wrist in a strong grip.

"That's all right," he said, with a great gasp of relief. "*Phew!* At one time I thought I had lost you."

"By heart-disease, or drowning?" inquired Miss Lindsay, softly.

Mr. Jobson awoke with a Sundayish feeling, probably due to the fact that it was Bank Holiday. He had been aware, in a dim fashion, of the rising of Mrs. Jobson some time before, and in a semi-conscious condition had taken over a large slice of unoccupied territory. He stretched himself and yawned, and then, by an effort of will, threw off the clothes and springing out of bed reached for his trousers.

He was an orderly man, and had hung them every night for over twenty years on the brass knob on his side of the bed. He had hung them there the night before, and now they had absconded with a pair of red braces just entering their teens. Instead, on a chair at the foot of the bed was a collection of garments that made him shudder. With trembling fingers he turned over a black tailcoat, a white waistcoat, and a pair of light check trousers. A white shirt, a collar, and tie kept them company, and, greatest outrage of all, a tall silk hat stood on its own band-box beside the chair. Mr. Jobson, fingering his bristly chin, stood: regarding the collection with a wan smile.

"So that's their little game, is it?" he muttered. "Want to make a toff of me. Where's my clothes got to, I wonder?"

A hasty search satisfied him that they were not in the room, and, pausing only to drape himself in the counterpane, he made his way into the next. He passed on to the others, and then, with a growing sense of alarm, stole softly downstairs and making his way to the shop continued the search. With the shutters up the place was almost in darkness, and in spite of his utmost care apples and potatoes rolled on to the floor and travelled across it in a succession of bumps. Then a sudden turn brought the scales clattering down.

"Good gracious, Alf!" said a voice. "Whatever are you a-doing of?"

Mr. Jobson turned and eyed his wife, who was standing at the door.

"I'm looking for my clothes, mother," he replied, briefly.

"Clothes!" said Mrs. Jobson, with an obvious attempt at unconcerned speech. "Clothes! Why, they're on the chair."

"I mean clothes fit for a Christian to wear—fit for a greengrocer to wear," said Mr. Jobson, raising his voice.

"It was a little surprise for you, dear," said his wife. "Me and Bert and Gladys and Dorothy 'ave all been saving up for it for ever so long."

"It's very kind of you all," said Mr. Jobson, feebly—"very, but—"

"They've all been doing without things themselves to do it," interjected his wife. "As for Gladys, I'm sure nobody knows what she's given up."

"Well, if nobody knows, it don't matter," said Mr. Jobson. "As I was saying, it's very kind of you all, but I can't wear 'em. Where's my others?"

Mrs. Jobson hesitated.

"Where's my others?" repeated her husband.

"They're being took care of," replied his wife, with spirit. "Aunt Emma's minding 'em for you—and you know what she is. H'sh! Alf! Alf! I'm surprised at you!"

Mr. Jobson coughed. "It's the collar, mother," he said at last. "I ain't wore a collar for over twenty years; not since we was walking out together. And then I didn't like it."

"More shame for you," said his wife. "I'm sure there's no other respectable tradesman goes about with a handkerchief knotted round his neck."

"P'r'aps their skins ain't as tender as what mine is," urged Mr. Jobson; "and besides, fancy me in a top-'at! Why, I shall be the laughing-stock of the place."

"Nonsense!" said his wife. "It's only the lower classes what would laugh, and nobody minds what they think."

Mr. Jobson sighed. "Well, I shall 'ave to go back to bed again, then," he said, ruefully. "So long, mother. Hope you have a pleasant time at the Palace."

He took a reef in the counterpane and with a fair amount of dignity, considering his appearance, stalked upstairs again and stood gloomily considering affairs in his bedroom. Ever since Gladys and Dorothy had been big enough to be objects of interest to the young men of the neighbourhood the clothes nuisance had been rampant. He peeped through the window-blind at the bright sunshine outside, and then looked back at the tumbled bed. A murmur of voices downstairs apprised him that the conspirators were awaiting the result.

He dressed at last and stood like a lamb—a redfaced, bull-necked lamb— while Mrs. Jobson fastened his collar for him.

"Bert wanted to get a taller one," she remarked, "but I said this would do to begin with."

"Wanted it to come over my mouth, I s'pose," said the unfortunate Mr. Jobson. "Well, 'ave it your own way. Don't mind about me. What with the trousers and the collar, I couldn't pick up a sovereign if I saw one in front of me."

"If you see one I'll pick it up for you," said his wife, taking up the hat and moving towards the door. "Come along!"

Mr. Jobson, with his arms standing out stiffly from his sides and his head painfully erect, followed her downstairs, and a sudden hush as he entered the kitchen testified to the effect produced by his appearance. It was followed by a hum of admiration that sent the blood flying to his head.

"Why he couldn't have done it before I don't know," said the dutiful Gladys. "Why, there ain't a man in the street looks a quarter as smart."

"Fits him like a glove!" said Dorothy, walking round him.

"Just the right length," said Bert, scrutinizing the coat.

"And he stands as straight as a soldier," said Gladys, clasping her hands gleefully.

"Collar," said Mr. Jobson, briefly. "Can I 'ave it took off while I eat my bloater, mother?"

"Don't be silly, Alf," said his wife. "Gladys, pour your father out a nice, strong, Pot cup o' tea, and don't forget that the train starts at ha' past ten."

"It'll start all right when it sees me," observed Mr. Jobson, squinting down at his trousers.

Mother and children, delighted with the success of their scheme, laughed applause, and Mr. Jobson somewhat gratified at the success of his retort, sat down and attacked his breakfast. A short clay pipe, smoked as a digestive, was impounded by the watchful Mrs. Jobson the moment he had finished it.

"He'd smoke it along the street if I didn't," she declared.

"And why not?" demanded her husband—always do."

"Not in a top-'at," said Mrs. Jobson, shaking her head at him.

"Or a tail-coat," said Dorothy.

"One would spoil the other," said Gladys.

"I wish something would spoil the hat," said Mr. Jobson, wistfully. "It's no good; I must smoke, mother."

Mrs. Jobson smiled, and, going to the cupboard, produced, with a smile of triumph, an envelope containing seven dangerous-looking cigars. Mr. Jobson whistled, and taking one up examined it carefully.

"What do they call 'em, mother?" he inquired. "The 'Cut and Try Again Smokes'?"

Mrs. Jobson smiled vaguely. "Me and the girls are going upstairs to get ready now," she said. "Keep your eye on him, Bert!"

Father and son grinned at each other, and, to pass the time, took a cigar apiece. They had just finished them when a swish and rustle of skirts sounded from the stairs, and Mrs. Jobson and the girls, beautifully attired, entered the room and stood buttoning their gloves. A strong smell of scent fought with the aroma of the cigars.

"You get round me like, so as to hide me a bit," entreated Mr. Jobson, as they quitted the house. "I don't mind so much when we get out of our street."

Mrs. Jobson laughed his fears to scorn.

"Well, cross the road, then," said Mr. Jobson, urgently. "There's Bill Foley standing at his door."

His wife sniffed. "Let him stand," she said, haughtily.

Mr. Foley failed to avail himself of the permission. He regarded Mr. Jobson with dilated eyeballs, and, as the party approached, sank slowly into a sitting position on his doorstep, and as the door opened behind him rolled slowly onto his back and presented an enormous pair of hobnailed soles to the gaze of an interested world.

"I told you 'ow it would be," said the blushing Mr. Jobson. "You know what Bill's like as well as I do."

His wife tossed her head and they all quickened their pace. The voice of the ingenious Mr. Foley calling piteously for his mother pursued them to the end of the road.

"I knew what it 'ud be," said Mr. Jobson, wiping his hot face. "Bill will never let me 'ear the end of this."

"Nonsense!" said his wife, bridling. "Do you mean to tell me you've got to ask Bill Foley 'ow you're to dress? He'll soon get tired of it; and, besides, it's just as well to let him see who you are. There's not many tradesmen as would lower themselves by mixing with a plasterer."

Mr. Jobson scratched his ear, but wisely refrained from speech. Once clear of his own district mental agitation subsided, but bodily discomfort increased at every step. The hat and the collar bothered him most, but every article of attire contributed its share. His uneasiness was so manifest that Mrs. Jobson, after a little womanly sympathy, suggested that, besides Sundays, it might be as well to wear them occasionally of an evening in order to get used to them.

"What, 'ave I got to wear them every Sunday?" demanded the unfortunate, blankly; "why, I thought they was only for Bank Holidays."

Mrs. Jobson told him not to be silly.

"Straight, I did," said her husband, earnestly. "You've no idea 'ow I'm suffering; I've got a headache, I'm arf choked, and there's a feeling about my waist as though I'm being cuddled by somebody I don't like."

Mrs. Jobson said it would soon wear off and, seated in the train that bore them to the Crystal Palace, put the hat on the rack. Her husband's attempt to leave it in the train was easily frustrated and his explanation that he had forgotten all about it received in silence. It was evident that he would require watching, and under the clear gaze of his children he seldom had a button undone for more than three minutes at a time.

The day was hot and he perspired profusely. His collar lost its starch— a thing to be grateful for— and for the greater part of the day he wore his tie under the left ear. By the time they had arrived home again he was in a state of open mutiny.

"Never again," he said, loudly, as he tore the collar off and hung his coat on a chair.

There was a chorus of lamentation; but he remained firm. Dorothy began to sniff ominously, and Gladys spoke longingly of the fathers possessed by other girls. It was not until Mrs. Jobson sat eyeing her supper, instead of eating it, that he began to temporize. He gave way bit by bit, garment by garment. When he gave way at last on the great hat question, his wife took up her knife and fork.

His workaday clothes appeared in his bedroom next morning, but the others still remained in the clutches of Aunt Emma. The suit provided was of considerable antiquity, and at closing time, Mr.

Jobson, after some hesitation, donned his new clothes and with a sheepish glance at his wife went out; Mrs. Jobson nodded delight at her daughters.

"He's coming round," she whispered. "He liked that ticket-collector calling him 'sir' yesterday. I noticed it. He's put on everything but the topper. Don't say nothing about it; take it as a matter of course."

It became evident as the days wore on that she was right... Bit by bit she obtained the other clothes—with some difficulty—from Aunt Emma, but her husband still wore his best on Sundays and sometimes of an evening; and twice, on going into the bedroom suddenly, she had caught him surveying himself at different angles in the glass.

And, moreover, he had spoken with some heat—for such a good-tempered man—on the shortcomings of Dorothy's laundry work.

"We'd better put your collars out," said his wife.

"And the shirts," said Mr. Jobson. "Nothing looks worse than a bad got-up cuff."

"You're getting quite dressy," said his wife, with a laugh.

Mr. Jobson eyed her seriously.

"No, mother, no," he replied. "All I've done is to find out that you're right, as you always 'ave been. A man in my persition has got no right to dress as if he kept a stall on the kerb. It ain't fair to the gals, or to young Bert. I don't want 'em to be ashamed of their father."

"They wouldn't be that," said Mrs. Jobson.

"I'm trying to improve," said her husband. "O' course, it's no use dressing up and behaving wrong, and yesterday I bought a book what tells you all about behaviour."

"Well done!" said the delighted Mrs. Jobson.

Mr. Jobson was glad to find that her opinion on his purchase was shared by the rest of the family. Encouraged by their approval, he told them of the benefit he was deriving from it; and at tea-time that day, after a little hesitation, ventured to affirm that it was a book that might do them all good.

"Hear, hear!" said Gladys.

"For one thing," said Mr. Jobson, slowly, "I didn't know before that it was wrong to blow your tea; and as for drinking it out of a saucer, the book says it's a thing that is only done by the lower orders."

"If you're in a hurry?" demanded Mr. Bert Jobson, pausing with his saucer half way to his mouth.

"If you're in anything," responded his father. "A gentleman would rather go without his tea than drink it out of a saucer. That's the sort o' thing Bill Foley would do."

Mr. Bert Jobson drained his saucer thoughtfully.

"Picking your teeth with your finger is wrong, too," said Mr. Jobson, taking a breath. "Food should be removed in a—a—un-undemonstrative fashion with the tip of the tongue."

"I wasn't," said Gladys.

"A knife," pursued her father—"a knife should never in any circumstances be allowed near the mouth."

"You've made mother cut herself," said Gladys, sharply; "that's what you've done."

"I thought it was my fork," said Mrs. Jobson. "I was so busy listening I wasn't thinking what I was doing. Silly of me."

"We shall all do better in time," said Mr. Jobson. "But what I want to know is, what about the gravy? You can't eat it with a fork, and it don't say nothing about a spoon. Oh, and what about our cold tubs, mother?"

"Cold tubs?" repeated his wife, staring at him. "What cold tubs?"

"The cold tubs me and Bert ought to 'ave," said Mr. Jobson. "It says in the book that an Englishman would just as soon think of going without his breakfus' as his cold tub; and you know how fond I am of my breakfus'."

"And what about me and the gals?" said the amazed Mrs. Jobson.

"Don't you worry about me, ma," said Gladys, hastily.

"The book don't say nothing about gals; it says Englishmen," said Mr. Jobson.

"But we ain't got a bathroom," said his son.

"It don't signify," said Mr. Jobson. "A washtub'll do. Me and Bert'll 'ave a washtub each brought up overnight; and it'll be exercise for the gals bringing the water up of a morning to us."

"Well, I don't know, I'm sure," said the bewildered Mrs. Jobson. "Anyway, you and Bert'll 'ave to carry the tubs up and down. Messy, I call it.

"It's got to be done, mother," said Mr. Jobson cheerfully. "It's only the lower orders what don't 'ave their cold tub reg'lar. The book says so."

He trundled the tub upstairs the same night and, after his wife had gone downstairs next morning, opened the door and took in the can and pail that stood outside. He poured the contents into the tub, and, after eyeing it thoughtfully for some time, agitated the surface with his right foot. He dipped and dried that much enduring member some ten times, and after regarding the damp condition of the towels with great satisfaction, dressed himself and went downstairs.

"I'm all of a glow," he said, seating himself at the table. "I believe I could eat a elephant. I feel as fresh as a daisy; don't you, Bert?"

Mr. Jobson, junior, who had just come in from the shop, remarked, shortly, that he felt more like a blooming snowdrop.

"And somebody slopped a lot of water over the stairs carrying it up," said Mrs. Jobson. "I don't believe as everybody has cold baths of a morning. It don't seem wholesome to me."

Mr. Jobson took a book from his pocket, and opening it at a certain page, handed it over to her.

"If I'm going to do the thing at all I must do it properly," he said, gravely. "I don't suppose Bill Foley ever 'ad a cold tub in his life; he don't know no better. Gladys!"

"Halloa!" said that young lady, with a start.

"Are you—are you eating that kipper with your fingers?"

Gladys turned and eyed her mother appealingly.

"Page-page one hundred and something, I think it is," said her father, with his mouth full. "'Manners at the Dinner Table.' It's near the end of the book, I know."

"If I never do no worse than that I shan't come to no harm," said his daughter.

Mr. Jobson shook his head at her, and after eating his breakfast with great care, wiped his mouth on his handkerchief and went into the shop.

"I suppose it's all right," said Mrs. Jobson, looking after him, "but he's taking it very serious—very."

"He washed his hands five times yesterday morning," said Dorothy, who had just come in from the shop to her breakfast; "and kept customers waiting while he did it, too."

"It's the cold-tub business I can't get over," said her mother. "I'm sure it's more trouble to empty them than what it is to fill them. There's quite enough work in the 'ouse as it is."

"Too much," said Bert, with unwonted consideration.

"I wish he'd leave me alone," said Gladys. "My food don't do me no good when he's watching every mouthful I eat."

Of murmurings such as these Mr. Jobson heard nothing, and in view of the great improvement in his dress and manners, a strong resolution was passed to avoid the faintest appearance of discontent. Even when, satisfied with his own appearance, he set to work to improve that of Mrs. Jobson, that admirable woman made no complaint. Hitherto the brightness of her attire and the size of her hats had been held to atone for her lack of figure and the roomy comfort of her boots, but Mr. Jobson, infected with new ideas, refused to listen to such sophistry. He went shopping with Dorothy; and the Sunday after, when Mrs. Jobson went for an airing with him, she walked in boots with heels two inches high and toes that ended in a point. A waist that had disappeared some years before was recaptured and placed in durance vile; and a hat which called for a new style of hair-dressing completed the effect.

"You look splendid, ma!" said Gladys, as she watched their departure. "Splendid!"

"I don't feel splendid," sighed Mrs. Jobson to her husband. "These 'ere boots feel red-'ot."

"Your usual size," said Mr. Jobson, looking across the road.

"And the clothes seem just a teeny-weeny bit tight, p'r'aps," continued his wife.

Mr. Jobson regarded her critically. "P'r'aps they might have been let out a quarter of an inch," he said, thoughtfully. "They're the best fit you've 'ad for a long time, mother. I only 'ope the gals'll 'ave such good figgers."

His wife smiled faintly, but, with little breath for conversation, walked on for some time in silence. A growing redness of face testified to her distress.

"I—I feel awful," she said at last, pressing her hand to her side. "Awful."

"You'll soon get used to it," said Mr. Jobson, gently. "Look at me! I felt like you do at first, and now I wouldn't go back to old clothes—and comfort—for anything. You'll get to love them boots.

"If I could only take 'em off I should love 'em better," said his wife, panting; "and I can't breathe properly—I can't breathe."

"You look ripping, mother," said her husband, simply.

His wife essayed another smile, but failed. She set her lips together and plodded on, Mr. Jobson chatting cheerily and taking no notice of the fact that she kept lurching against him. Two miles from home she stopped and eyed him fixedly.

"If I don't get these boots off, Alf, I shall be a 'elpless cripple for the rest of my days," she murmured. "My ankle's gone over three times."

"But you can't take 'em off here," said Mr. Jobson, hastily. "Think 'ow it would look."

"I must 'ave a cab or something," said his wife, hysterically. "If I don't get 'em off soon I shall scream."

She leaned against the iron palings of a house for support, while Mr. Jobson, standing on the kerb, looked up and down the road for a cab. A four-wheeler appeared just in time to prevent the scandal—of Mrs. Jobson removing her boots in the street.

"Thank goodness," she gasped, as she climbed in. "Never mind about untying 'em, Alf; cut the laces and get 'em off quick."

They drove home with the boots standing side by side on the seat in front of them. Mr. Jobson got out first and knocked at the door, and as soon as it opened Mrs. Jobson pattered across the intervening space with the boots dangling from her hand. She had nearly reached the door when Mr. Foley, who had a diabolical habit of always being on hand when he was least wanted, appeared suddenly from the offside of the cab.

"Been paddlin'?" he inquired.

Mrs. Jobson, safe in her doorway, drew herself up and, holding the boots behind her, surveyed him with a stare of high-bred disdain.

"Been paddlin'?" he inquired

"I see you going down the road in 'em," said the unabashed Mr. Foley, "and I says to myself, I says, 'Pride'll bear a pinch, but she's going too far. If she thinks that she can squeedge those little tootsywootsies of 'ers into them boo—'"

The door slammed violently and left him exchanging grins with Mr. Jobson.

"How's the 'at?" he inquired.

Mr. Jobson winked. "Bet you a level 'arf-dollar I ain't wearing it next Sunday," he said, in a hoarse whisper.

Mr. Foley edged away.

"Not good enough," he said, shaking his head. "I've had a good many bets with you first and last, Alf, but I can't remember as I ever won one yet. So long."

FOR BETTER OR WORSE

Mr. George Wotton, gently pushing the swing doors of the public bar of the "King's Head" an inch apart, applied an eye to the aperture, in the hope of discovering a moneyed friend. His gaze fell on the only man in the bar a greybeard of sixty whose weather-beaten face and rough clothing spoke of the sea. With a faint sigh he widened the opening and passed through.

"Mornin', Ben," he said, with an attempt at cheerfulness.

"Have a drop with me," said the other, heartily. "Got any money about you?"

Mr. Wotton shook his head and his face fell, clearing somewhat as the other handed him his mug. "Drink it all up, George," he said.

His friend complied. A more tactful man might have taken longer over the job, but Mr. Benjamin Davis, who appeared to be labouring under some strong excitement, took no notice.

"I've had a shock, George," he said, regarding the other steadily. "I've heard news of my old woman."

"Didn't know you 'ad one," said Mr. Wotton calmly. "Wot's she done?"

"She left me," said Mr. Davis, solemnly—"she left me thirty-five years ago. I went off to sea one fine morning, and that was the last I ever see of er.

"Why, did she bolt?" inquired Mr. Wotton, with mild interest.

"No," said his friend, "but I did. We'd been married three years—three long years—and I had 'ad enough of it. Awful temper she had. The last words I ever heard 'er say was: 'Take that!'"

Mr. Wotton took up the mug and, after satisfying himself as to the absence of contents, put it down again and yawned.

"I shouldn't worry about it if I was you," he remarked. "She's hardly likely to find you now. And if she does she won't get much."

Mr. Davis gave vent to a contemptuous laugh. "Get much!" he repeated. "It's her what's got it. I met a old shipmate of mine this morning what I 'adn't seen for ten years, and he told me he run acrost 'er only a month ago. After she left me—"

"But you said you left her!" exclaimed his listening friend.

"Same thing," said Mr. Davis, impatiently. "After she left me to work myself to death at sea, running here and there at the orders of a pack o'lazy scuts aft, she went into service and stayed in one place for fifteen years. Then 'er missis died and left her all 'er money. For twenty years, while I've been working myself to skin and bone, she's been living in comfort and idleness."

"'Ard lines," said Mr. Wotton, shaking his head. "It don't bear thinking of."

"Why didn't she advertise for me?" said Mr. Davis, raising his voice. "That's what I want to know. Advertisements is cheap enough; why didn't she advertise? I should 'ave come at once if she'd said anything about money."

Mr. Wotton shook his head again. "P'r'aps she didn't want you," he said, slowly.

"What's that got to do with it?" demanded the other. "It was 'er dooty. She'd got money, and I ought to have 'ad my 'arf of it. Nothing can make up for that wasted twenty years—nothing."

"P'r'aps she'll take you back," said Mr. Wotton.

"Take me back?" repeated Mr. Davis. "O' course she'll take me back. She'll have to. There's a law in the land, ain't there? What I'm thinking of is: Can I get back my share what I ought to have 'ad for the last twenty years?"

"Get 'er to take you back first," counselled his friend. "Thirty-five years is a long time, and p'r'aps she has lost 'er love for you. Was you good-looking in those days?"

"Yes," snapped Mr. Davis; "I ain't altered much—. 'Sides, what about her?"

"That ain't the question," said the other. "She's got a home and money. It don't matter about looks; and, wot's more, she ain't bound to keep you. If you take my advice, you won't dream of letting her know you run away from her. Say you was cast away at sea, and when you came back years afterwards you couldn't find her."

Mr. Davis pondered for some time in sulky silence.

"P'r'aps it would be as well," he said at last; "but I sha'n't stand no nonsense, mind."

"If you like I'll come with you," said Mr. Wotton. "I ain't got nothing to do. I could tell 'er I was cast away with you if you liked. Anything to help a pal."

Mr. Davis took two inches of soiled clay pipe from his pocket and puffed thoughtfully.

"You can come," he said at last. "If you'd only got a copper or two we could ride; it's down Clapham way."

Mr. Wotton smiled feebly, and after going carefully through his pockets shook his head and followed his friend outside.

"I wonder whether she'll be pleased?" he remarked, as they walked slowly along. "She might be—women are funny creatures—so faithful. I knew one whose husband used to knock 'er about dreadful, and after he died she was so true to his memory she wouldn't marry again."

Mr. Davis grunted, and, with a longing eye at the omnibuses passing over London Bridge, asked a policeman the distance to Clapham.

"Never mind," said Mr. Wotton, as his friend uttered an exclamation. "You'll have money in your pocket soon."

Mr. Davis's face brightened. "And a watch and chain too," he said.

"And smoke your cigar of a Sunday," said Mr. Wotton, "and have a easy-chair and a glass for a friend."

Mr. Davis almost smiled, and then, suddenly remembering his wasted twenty years, shook his head grimly over the friendship that attached itself to easy-chairs and glasses of ale, and said that there was plenty of it about. More friendship than glasses of ale and easy-chairs, perhaps.

At Clapham, they inquired the way of a small boy, and, after following the road indicated, retraced their steps, cheered by a faint but bloodthirsty hope of meeting him again.

A friendly baker put them on the right track at last, both gentlemen eyeing the road with a mixture of concern and delight. It was a road of trim semi-detached villas, each with a well-kept front garden and neatly-curtained windows. At the gate of a house with the word "Blairgowrie" inscribed in huge gilt letters on the fanlight Mr. Davis paused for a moment uneasily, and then, walking up the path, followed by Mr. Wotton, knocked at the door.

He retired a step in disorder before the apparition of a maid in cap and apron. A sharp "Not to-day!" sounded in his ears and the door closed again. He faced his friend gasping.

"I should give her the sack first thing," said Mr. Wotton.

Mr. Davis knocked again, and again. The maid reappeared, and after surveying them through the glass opened the door a little way and parleyed.

"I want to see your missis," said Mr. Davis, fiercely.

"What for?" demanded the girl.

"You tell 'er," said Mr. Davis, inserting his foot just in time, "you tell 'er that there's two gentlemen here what have brought 'er news of her husband, and look sharp about it."

"They was cast away with 'im," said Mr. Wotton.

"On a desert island," said Mr. Davis. He pushed his way in, followed by his friend, and a head that had been leaning over the banisters was suddenly withdrawn. For a moment he stood irresolute in the tiny passage, and then, with a husband's boldness, he entered the front room and threw himself into an easy-chair. Mr. Wotton, after a scared glance around the well-furnished room, seated himself on the extreme edge of the most uncomfortable chair he could find and coughed nervously.

"Better not be too sudden with her," he whispered. "You don't want her to faint, or anything of that sort. Don't let 'er know who you are at first; let her find it out for herself."

Mr. Davis, who was also suffering from the stiff grandeur of his surroundings, nodded.

"P'r'aps you'd better start, in case she reckernizes my voice," he said, slowly. "Pitch it in strong about me and 'ow I was always wondering what had 'appened to her."

"You're in luck, that's wot you are," said his friend, enviously. "I've only seen furniture like thiss in shop windows before. H'sh! Here she comes."

He started, and both men tried to look at their ease as a stiff rustling sounded from the stairs. Then the door opened and a tall, stoutly-built old lady with white hair swept into the room and stood regarding them.

Mr. Davis, unprepared for the changes wrought by thirty-five years, stared at her aghast. The black silk dress, the gold watch-chain, and huge cameo brooch did not help to reassure him.

"Good-good afternoon, ma'am," said Mr. Wotton, in a thin voice.

The old lady returned the greeting, and, crossing to a chair and seating herself in a very upright fashion, regarded him calmly.

"We—we called to see you about a dear old pal—friend, I mean," continued Mr. Wotton; "one o' the best. The best."

"Yes?" said the old lady.

"He's been missing," said Mr. Wotton, watching closely for any symptoms of fainting, "for thir-ty-five years. Thir-ty-five years ago-very much against his wish-he left 'is young and handsome wife to go for a sea v'y'ge, and was shipwrecked and cast away on a desert island."

"Yes?" said the old lady again.

"I was cast away with 'im," said Mr. Wotton. "Both of us was cast away with him."

He indicated Mr. Davis with his hand, and the old lady, after a glance at that gentleman, turned to Mr. Wotton again.

"We was on that island for longer than I like to think of," continued Mr. Wotton, who had a wholesome dread of dates. "But we was rescued at last, and ever since then he has been hunting high and low for his wife."

"It's very interesting," murmured the old lady; "but what has it got to do with me?"

Mr. Wotton gasped, and cast a helpless glance at his friend.

"You ain't heard his name yet," he said, impressively. "Wot would you say if I said it was—Ben Davis?"

"I should say it wasn't true," said the old lady, promptly.

"Not—true?" said Mr. Wotton, catching his breath painfully. "Wish I may die—"

"About the desert island," continued the old lady, calmly. "The story that I heard was that he went off like a cur and left his young wife to do the best she could for herself. I suppose he's heard since that she has come in for a bit of money."

"Money!" repeated Mr. Wotton, in a voice that he fondly hoped expressed artless surprise. "Money!"

"Money," said the old lady; "and I suppose he sent you two gentlemen round to see how the land lay."

She was looking full at Mr. Davis as she spoke, and both men began to take a somewhat sombre view of the situation.

"You didn't know him, else you wouldn't talk like that," said Mr. Wotton. "I don't suppose you'd know 'im if you was to see him now."

"I don't suppose I should," said the other.

"P'r'aps you'd reckernize his voice?" said Mr. Davis, breaking silence at last.

Mr. Wotton held his breath, but the old lady merely shook her head thoughtfully. "It was a disagreeable voice when his wife used to hear it," she said at last. "Always fault-finding, when it wasn't swearing."

Mr. Wotton glanced at his friend, and, raising his eyebrows slightly, gave up his task. "Might ha' been faults on both sides," said Mr. Davis, gruffly. "You weren't all that you should ha' been, you know."

"Me!" said his hostess, raising her voice.

"Yes, you," said Mr. Davis, rising. "Don't you know me, Mary? Why, I knew you the moment you come into the room."

He moved towards her awkwardly, but she rose in her turn and drew back.

"If you touch me I'll scream," she said, firmly. "How dare you. Why, I've never seen you before in my life."

"It's Ben Davis, ma'am; it's 'im, right enough," said Mr. Wotton, meekly.

"Hold your tongue," said the old lady.

"Look at me!" commanded Mr. Davis, sternly. "Look at me straight in the eye."

"Don't talk nonsense," said the other, sharply. "Look you in the eye, indeed! I don't want to look in your eye. What would people think?"

"Let 'em think wot they like," said Mr. Davis, recklessly. "This is a nice home-coming after being away thirty-five years."

"Most of it on a desert island," put in Mr. Wotton, pathetically.

"And now I've come back," resumed Mr. Davis; "come back to stop."

He hung his cap on a vase on the mantelpiece that reeled under the shock, and, dropping into his chair again, crossed his legs and eyed her sternly. Her gaze was riveted on his dilapidated boots. She looked up and spoke mildly.

"You're not my husband," she said. "You've made a mistake—I think you had better go."

"Ho!" said Mr. Davis, with a hard laugh. "Indeed! And 'ow do you know I'm not?"

"For the best of reasons," was the reply. "Besides, how can you prove that you are? Thirty-five years is a long time."

"'Specially on a desert island," said Mr. Wotton, rapidly. "You'd be surprised 'ow slow the time passes. I was there with 'im, and I can lay my hand on my 'art and assure you that that is your husband."

"Nonsense!" said the old lady, vigorously. "Rubbish!"

"I can prove it," said Mr. Davis, fixing her with a glittering eye. "Do you remember the serpent I 'ad tattooed on my leg for a garter?"

"If you don't go at once," said the old lady, hastily, "I'll send for the police."

"You used to admire it," said Mr. Davis, reproachfully. "I remember once—"

"If you say another word," said the other, in a fierce voice, "I'll send straight off for the police. You and your serpents! I'll tell my husband of you, that's what I'll do."

"Your WHAT?" roared Mr. Davis, springing to his feet.

"My husband. He won't stand any of your nonsense, I can tell you. You'd better go before he comes in."

"O-oh," said Mr. Davis, taking a long breath. "Oh, so you been and got married again, 'ave you? That's your love for your husband as was cast away while trying to earn a living for you. That's why you don't want me, is it? We'll see. I'll wait for him."

"You don't know what you're talking about," said the other, with great dignity. "I've only been married once."

Mr. Davis passed the back of his hand across his eyes in a dazed fashion and stared at her.

"Is—is somebody passing himself off as me?" he demanded. "'Cos if he is I'll 'ave you both up for bigamy."

"Certainly not."

"But—but—"

Mr. Davis turned and looked blankly at his friend. Mr. Wotton met his gaze with dilated eyes.

"You say you recognize me as your wife?" said the old lady.

"Certainly," said Mr. Davis, hotly.

"It's very curious," said the other—"very. But are you sure? Look again."

Mr. Davis thrust his face close to hers and stared hard. She bore his scrutiny without flinching.

"I'm positive certain," said Mr. Davis, taking a breath.

"That's very curious," said the old lady; "but, then, I suppose we are a bit alike. You see, Mrs. Davis being away, I'm looking after her house for a bit. My name happens to be Smith."

Mr. Davis uttered a sharp exclamation, and, falling back a step, stared at her open-mouthed.

"We all make mistakes," urged Mr. Wotton, after a long silence, "and Ben's sight ain't wot it used to be. He strained it looking out for a sail when we was on that desert—"

"When—when'll she be back?" inquired Mr. Davis, finding his voice at last.

The old lady affected to look puzzled. "But I thought you were certain that I was your wife?" she said, smoothly.

"My mistake," said Mr. Davis, ruefully. "Thirty-five years is a long time and people change a bit; I have myself. For one thing, I must say I didn't expect to find 'er so stout."

"Stout!" repeated the other, quickly.

"Not that I mean you're too stout," said Mr. Davis, hurriedly—"for people that like stoutness, that is. My wife used to 'ave a very good figger."

Mr. Wotton nodded. "He used to rave about it on that des—"

"When will she be back?" inquired Mr. Davis, interrupting him.

Mrs. Smith shook her head. "I can't say," she replied, moving towards the door. "When she's off holidaying, I never know when she'll return. Shall I tell her you called?"

"Tell her I—certainly," said Mr. Davis, with great vehemence. "I'll come in a week's time and see if she's back."

"She might be away for months," said the old lady, moving slowly to the passage and opening the street door. "Good-afternoon."

She closed the door behind them and stood watching them through the glass as they passed disconsolately into the street. Then she went back into the parlour, and standing before the mantelpiece, looked long and earnestly into the mirror.

Mr. Davis returned a week later—alone, and, pausing at the gate, glanced in dismay at a bill in the window announcing that the house was to be sold. He walked up the path still looking at it, and being admitted by the trim servant was shown into the parlour, and stood in a dispirited fashion before Mrs. Smith.

"Not back yet?" he inquired, gruffly.

The old lady shook her head.

"What—what—is that bill for?" demanded Mr. Davis, jerking his thumb towards it.

"She is thinking of selling the house," said Mrs. Smith. "I let her know you had been, and that is, the result. She won't comeback. You won't see her again."

"Where is she?" inquired Mr. Davis, frowning.

Mrs. Smith shook her head again. "And it would be no use my telling you," she said. "What she has got is her own, and the law won't let you touch a penny of it without her consent. You must have treated her badly; why did you leave her?"

"Why?" repeated Mr. Davis. "Why? Why, because she hit me over the 'ead with a broom-handle."

Mrs. Smith tossed her head.

"Fancy you remembering that for thirty-five years!" she said.

"Fancy forgetting it!" retorted Mr. Davis.

"I suppose she had a hot temper," said the old lady.

"'Ot temper?" said the other. "Yes." He leaned forward, and holding his chilled hands over the fire stood for some time deep in thought.

"I don't know what it is," he said at last, "but there's a something about you that reminds me of her. It ain't your voice, 'cos she had a very nice voice—when she wasn't in a temper—and it ain't your face, because—"

"Yes?" said Mrs. Smith, sharply. "Because it don't remind me of her."

"And yet the other day you said you recognized me at once," said the old lady.

"I thought I did," said Mr. Davis. "One thing is, I was expecting to see her, I s'pose."

There was a long silence.

"Well, I won't keep you," said Mrs. Smith at last, "and it's no good for you to keep coming here to see her. She will never come here again. I don't want to hurt your feelings, but you don't look over and above respectable. Your coat is torn, your trousers are patched in a dozen places, and your boots are half off your feet—I don't know what the servant must think."

"I—I only came to look for my wife," said Mr. Davis, in a startled voice. "I won't come again."

"That's right," said the old lady. "That'll please her, I know. And if she should happen to ask what sort of a living you are making, what shall I tell her?"

"Tell her what you said about my clothes, ma'am," said Mr. Davis, with his hand on the door-knob. "She'll understand then. She's known wot it is to be poor herself. She'd got a bad temper, but she'd have cut her tongue out afore she'd 'ave thrown a poor devil's rags in his face. Good-afternoon."

"Good-afternoon, Ben," said the old woman, in a changed voice.

Mr. Davis, half-way through the door, started as though he had been shot, and, facing about, stood eyeing her in dumb bewilderment.

"If I take you back again," repeated his wife, "are you going to behave yourself?"

"It isn't the same voice and it isn't the same face," said the old woman; "but if I'd only got a broomhandle handy—"

Mr. Davis made an odd noise in his throat.

"If you hadn't been so down on your luck," said his wife, blinking her eyes rapidly, "I'd have let you go. If you hadn't looked 'so miserable I could have stood it. If I take you back, are you going to behave yourself?"

Mr. Davis stood gaping at her.

"If I take you back again," repeated his wife, speaking very slowly, "are you going to behave yourself?"

"Yes," said Mr. Davis, finding his voice at last. "Yes, if you are."

THE FOUR PIGEONS

The old man took up his mug and shifted along the bench until he was in the shade of the elms that stood before the *Cauliflower*. The action also had the advantage of bringing him opposite the two strangers who were refreshing themselves after the toils of a long walk in the sun.

"My hearing ain't wot it used to be," he said, tremulously. "When you asked me to have a mug o' ale

I 'ardly heard you; and if you was to ask me to 'ave another, I mightn't hear you at all."

One of the men nodded.

"Not over there," piped the old man. "That's why I come over here," he added, after a pause. "It 'ud be rude like to take no notice; if you was to ask me."

He looked round as the landlord approached, and pushed his mug gently in his direction. The landlord, obeying a nod from the second stranger, filled it.

"It puts life into me," said the old man, raising it to his lips and bowing. "It makes me talk."

"Time we were moving, Jack," said the first traveller. The second, assenting to this as an abstract proposition, expressed, however, a determination to finish his pipe first.

I heard you saying something about shooting, continued the old man, and that reminds me of some shooting we 'ad here once in Claybury. We've always 'ad a lot o' game in these parts, and if it wasn't for a low, poaching fellow named Bob Pretty—Claybury's disgrace I call 'im—we'd 'ave a lot more.

It happened in this way. Squire Rockett was going abroad to foreign parts for a year, and he let the Hall to a gentleman from London named Sutton. A real gentleman 'e was, open-'anded and free, and just about October he 'ad a lot of 'is friends come down from London to 'elp 'im kill the pheasants.

The first day they frightened more than they killed, but they enjoyed theirselves all right until one gentleman, who 'adn't shot a single thing all day, shot pore Bill Chambers wot was beating with about a dozen more.

Bill got most of it in the shoulder and a little in the cheek, but the row he see fit to make you'd ha' thought he'd been killed. He laid on the ground groaning with 'is eyes shut, and everybody thought 'e was dying till Henery Walker stooped down and asked 'im whether 'e was hurt.

It took four men to carry Bill 'ome, and he was that particular you wouldn't believe. They 'ad to talk in whispers, and when Peter Gubbins forgot 'imself and began to whistle he asked him where his 'art was. When they walked fast he said they jolted 'im, and when they walked slow 'e asked 'em whether they'd gone to sleep or wot.

Bill was in bed for nearly a week, but the gentleman was very nice about it and said that it was his fault. He was a very pleasant-spoken gentleman, and, arter sending Dr. Green to him and saying he'd pay the bill, 'e gave Bill Chambers ten pounds to make up for 'is sufferings.

Bill 'ad intended to lay up for another week, and the doctor, wot 'ad been calling twice a day, said he wouldn't be responsible for 'is life if he didn't; but the ten pounds was too much for 'im, and one evening, just a week arter the accident, he turned up at this *Cauliflower* public-'ouse and began to spend 'is money.

His face was bandaged up, and when 'e come in he walked feeble-like and spoke in a faint sort o' voice. Smith, the landlord, got 'im a easy-chair and a couple of pillers out o' the parlour, and Bill sat there like a king, telling us all his sufferings and wot it felt like to be shot.

I always have said wot a good thing beer is, and it done Bill more good than doctor's medicine. When he came in he could 'ardly crawl, and at nine o'clock 'e was out of the easy-chair and dancing on the table as well as possible. He smashed three mugs and upset about two pints o' beer, but he just put his 'and in his pocket and paid for 'em without a word.

"There's plenty more where that came from," he ses, pulling out a handful o' money.

Peter Gubbins looked at it, 'ardly able to speak. "It's worth while being shot to 'ave all that money," he ses, at last.

"Don't you worry yourself, Peter," ses Bob Pretty; "there's plenty more of you as'll be shot afore them gentlemen at the Hall 'as finished. Bill's the fust, but 'e won't be the last—not by a long chalk."

"They're more careful now," ses Dicky Weed, the tailor.

"All right; 'ave it your own way," ses Bob, nasty-like. "I don't know much about shooting, being on'y a pore labourin' man. All I know is I shouldn't like to go beating for them. I'm too fond o' my wife and family."

"There won't be no more shot," ses Sam Jones.

"We're too careful," ses Peter Gubbins.

"Bob Pretty don't know everything," ses Dicky Weed.

"I'll bet you what you like there'll be some more of you shot," ses Bob Pretty, in a temper. "Now, then."

"'Ow much'll you bet, Bob," ses Sam Jones, with a wink at the others. "I can see you winking, Sam Jones," ses Bob Pretty, "but I'll do more than bet. The last bet I won is still owing to me. Now, look 'ere; I'll pay you sixpence a week all the time you're beating if you promise to give me arf of wot you get if you're shot. I can't say fairer than that."

"Will you give me sixpence a week, too?" ses Henery Walker, jumping up.

"I will," ses Bob; "and anybody else that likes. And wot's more, I'll pay in advance. Fust sixpences now."

Claybury men 'ave never been backward when there's been money to be made easy, and they all wanted to join Bob Pretty's club, as he called it. But fust of all 'e asked for a pen and ink, and then he got Smith, the land-lord, being a scholard, to write out a paper for them to sign. Henery Walker was the fust to write 'is name, and then Sam Jones, Peter Gubbins, Ralph Thomson, Jem Hall, and Walter Bell wrote theirs. Bob stopped 'em then, and said six 'ud be enough to go on with; and then 'e paid up the sixpences and wished 'em luck.

Wot they liked a'most as well as the sixpences was the idea o' getting the better o' Bob Pretty. As I said afore, he was a poacher, and that artful that up to that time nobody 'ad ever got the better of 'im.

They made so much fun of 'im the next night that Bob turned sulky and went off 'ome, and for two or three nights he 'ardly showed his face; and the next shoot they 'ad he went off to Wickham and nobody saw 'im all day.

That very day Henery Walker was shot. Several gentlemen fired at a rabbit that was started, and the next thing they knew Henery Walker was lying on the ground calling out that 'is leg 'ad been shot off.

He made more fuss than Bill Chambers a'most, 'specially when they dropped 'im off a hurdle carrying him 'ome, and the things he said to Dr. Green for rubbing his 'ands as he came into the bedroom was disgraceful.

The fust Bob Pretty 'eard of it was up at the *Cauliflower* at eight o'clock that evening, and he set down 'is beer and set off to see Henery as fast as 'is legs could carry 'im. Henery was asleep when 'e got there, and, do all he could, Bob Pretty couldn't wake 'im till he sat down gentle on 'is bad leg.

"It's on'y me, old pal," he ses, smiling at 'im as Henery woke up and shouted at 'im to get up.

Henery Walker was going to say something bad, but 'e thought better of it, and he lay there arf busting with rage, and watching Bob out of the corner of one eye.

"I quite forgot you was on my club till Smith reminded me of it," ses Bob. "Don't you take a farthing less than ten pounds, Henery."

Henery Walker shut his eyes again. "I forgot to tell you I made up my mind this morning not to belong to your club any more, Bob," he ses.

"Why didn't you come and tell me, Henery, instead of leaving it till it was too late?" ses Bob, shaking his 'ead at 'im.

"I shall want all that money," ses Henery in a weak voice. "I might 'ave to have a wooden leg, Bob."

"Don't meet troubles arf way, Henery," ses Bob, in a kind voice. "I've no doubt Mr. Sutton'll throw in a wooden leg if you want it, and look here, if he does, I won't trouble you for my arf of it."

He said good-night to Henery and went off, and when Mrs. Walker went up to see 'ow Henery was getting on he was carrying on that alarming that she couldn't do nothing with 'im.

He was laid up for over a week, though it's my opinion he wasn't much hurt, and the trouble was that nobody knew which gentleman 'ad shot 'im. Mr. Sutton talked it over with them, and at last, arter a good deal o' trouble, and Henery pulling up 'is trousers and showing them 'is leg till they was fair sick of the sight of it, they paid 'im ten pounds, the same as they 'ad Bill.

It took Bob Pretty two days to get his arf, but he kept very quiet about it, not wishing to make a fuss in the village for fear Mr. Sutton should get to hear of the club. At last he told Henery Walker that 'e was going to Wickham to see 'is lawyer about it, and arter Smith the landlord 'ad read the paper to Henery and explained 'ow he'd very likely 'ave to pay more than the whole ten pounds then, 'e gave Bob his arf and said he never wanted to see 'im again as long as he lived.

Bob stood treat up at the *Cauliflower* that night, and said 'ow bad he'd been treated. The tears stood in 'is eyes a'most, and at last 'e said that if 'e thought there was going to be any more fuss of that kind he'd wind up the club.

"It's the best thing you can do," ses Sam Jones; "I'm not going to belong to it any longer, so I give you notice. If so be as I get shot I want the money for myself."

"Me, too," ses Peter Gubbins; "it 'ud fair break my 'art to give Bob Pretty five pounds. I'd sooner give it to my wife."

All the other chaps said the same thing, but Bob pointed out to them that they 'ad taken their sixpences on'y the night afore, and they must stay in for the week. He said that was the law. Some of 'em talked about giving 'im 'is sixpences back, but Bob said if they did they must pay up all the sixpences they had 'ad for three weeks. The end of it was they said they'd stay in for that week and not a moment longer.

The next day Sam Jones and Peter Gubbins altered their minds. Sam found a couple o' shillings that his wife 'ad hidden in her Sunday bonnet, and Peter Gubbins opened 'is boy's money-box to see 'ow much there was in it. They came up to the *Cauliflower* to pay Bob their eighteen-pences, but he wasn't there, and when they went to his 'ouse Mrs. Pretty said as 'ow he'd gone off to Wickham and wouldn't be back till Saturday. So they 'ad to spend the money on beer instead.

That was on Tuesday, and things went on all right till Friday, when Mr. Sutton 'ad another shoot. The birds was getting scarce and the gentlemen that anxious to shoot them there was no 'olding them. Once or twice the keepers spoke to 'em about carefulness, and said wot large families they'd got, but it wasn't much good. They went on blazing away, and just at the corner of the wood Sam Jones and Peter Gubbins was both hit; Sam in the leg and Peter in the arm.

The noise that was made was awful—everybody shouting that they 'adn't done it, and all speaking at once, and Mr. Sutton was dancing about a'most beside 'imself with rage. Pore Sam and Peter was 'elped along by the others; Sam being carried and Peter led, and both of 'em with the idea of getting all they could out of it, making such 'orrible noises that Mr. Sutton couldn't hear 'imself calling his friends names.

"There seems to be wounded men calling out all over the place," he ses, in a temper.

"I think there is another one over there, sir," ses one o' the keepers, pointing.

Sam Jones and Peter Gubbins both left off to listen, and then they all heard it distinctly. A dreadful noise it was, and when Mr. Sutton and one or two more follered it up they found poor Walter Bell lying on 'is face in a bramble.

"Wot's the matter?" ses Mr. Sutton, shouting at 'im.

"I've been shot from behind," ses Walter. "I'd got something in my boot, and I was just stooping down to fasten it up agin when I got it.

"But there oughtn't to be anybody 'ere," ses Mr. Sutton to one of the keepers.

"They get all over the place, sir," ses the 'keeper, scratching his 'ead. "I fancied I 'eard a gun go off here a minute or two arter the others was shot."

"I believe he's done it 'imself," says Mr. Sutton, stamping his foot.

"I don't see 'ow he could, sir," ses the keeper, touching his cap and looking at Walter as was still lying with 'is face on 'is arms.

They carried Walter 'ome that way on a hurdle, and Dr. Green spent all the rest o' that day picking shots out o' them three men and telling 'em to keep still. He 'ad to do Sam Jones by candle-light, with Mrs. Jones 'olding the candle with one hand and crying with the other. Twice the doctor told her to keep it steady, and poor Sam 'ad only just passed the remark, "How 'ot it was for October," when they discovered that the bed was on fire. The doctor said that Sam was no trouble. He got off of the bed by 'imself, and, when it was all over and the fire put out, the doctor found him sitting on the stairs with the leg of a broken chair in 'is hand calling for 'is wife.

Of course, there was a terrible to-do about it in Claybury, and up at the Hall, too. All of the gentlemen said as 'ow they hadn't done it, and Mr. Sutton was arf crazy with rage. He said that they 'ad made 'im the laughing-stock of the neighbourhood, and that they oughtn't to shoot with anything but pop-guns. They got to such high words over it that two of the gentlemen went off 'ome that very night.

There was a lot of talk up at the *Cauliflower,* too, and more than one pointed out 'ow lucky Bob Pretty was in getting four men out of the six in his club. As I said afore, Bob was away at the time, but he came back the next night and we 'ad the biggest row here you could wish for to see.

Henery Walker began it. "I s'pose you've 'eard the dreadful news, Bob Pretty?" he ses, looking at 'im.

"I 'ave." ses Bob; "and my 'art bled for 'em. I told you wot those gentlemen was like, didn't I? But none of you would believe me. Now you can see as I was right."

"It's very strange," ses Henery Walker, looking round; "it's very strange that all of us wot's been shot belonged to Bob Pretty's precious club."

"It's my luck, Henery," ses Bob, "always was lucky from a child."

"And I s'pose you think you're going to 'ave arf of the money they get?" ses Henery Walker.

"Don't talk about money while them pore chaps is suffering," ses Bob. "I'm surprised at you, Henery."

"You won't 'ave a farthing of it," ses Henery Walker; "and wot's more, Bob Pretty, I'm going to 'ave my five pounds back."

"Don't you believe it, Henery," ses Bob, smiling at 'im.

"I'm going to 'ave my five pounds back," ses Henery, "and you know why. I know wot your club was for now, and we was all a pack o' silly fools not to see it afore."

"Speak for yourself, Henery," ses John Biggs, who thought Henery was looking at 'im.

"I've been putting two and two together," ses Henery, looking round, "and it's as plain as the nose on your face. Bob Pretty hid up in the wood and shot us all himself!"

For a moment you might 'ave heard a pin drop, and then there was such a noise nobody could hear theirselves speak. Everybody was shouting his 'ardest, and the on'y quiet one there was Bob Pretty 'imself.

"Poor Henery; he's gorn mad," he ses, shaking his 'ead.

"You're a murderer," ses Ralph Thomson, shaking 'is fist at him.

"Henery Walker's gorn mad," ses Bob agin. "Why, I ain't been near the place. There's a dozen men'll swear that I was at Wickham each time these misfortunate accidents 'appened."

"Men like you, they'd swear anything for a pot o' beer," ses Henery. "But I'm not going to waste time talking to you, Bob Pretty. I'm going straight off to tell Mr. Sutton."

"I shouldn't do that if I was you, Henery," ses Bob.

"I dessay," ses Henery Walker; "but then you see I am."

"I thought you'd gorn mad, Henery," ses Bob, taking a drink o' beer that somebody 'ad left on the table by mistake, "and now I'm sure of it. Why, if you tell Mr. Sutton that it wasn't his friends that shot them pore fellers he won't pay them anything. 'Tain't likely 'e would, is it?"

Henery Walker, wot 'ad been standing up looking fierce at 'im, sat down agin, struck all of a heap.

"And he might want your ten pounds back, Henery," said Bob in a soft voice. "And seeing as 'ow you was kind enough to give five to me, and spent most of the other, it 'ud come 'ard on you, wouldn't it? Always think afore you speak, Henery. I always do."

Henery Walker got up and tried to speak, but 'e couldn't, and he didn't get 'is breath back till Bob said it was plain to see that he 'adn't got a word to say for 'imself. Then he shook 'is fist at Bob and called 'im a low, thieving, poaching murderer.

"You're not yourself, Henery," ses Bob. "When you come round you'll be sorry for trying to take away the character of a pore labourin' man with a ailing wife and a large family. But if you take my advice you won't say anything more about your wicked ideas; if you do, these pore fellers won't get a farthing. And you'd better keep quiet about the club mates for their sakes. Other people might get the same crazy ideas in their silly 'eads as Henery. Keepers especially."

That was on'y common sense; but, as John Biggs said, it did seem 'ard to think as 'ow Bob Pretty should be allowed to get off scot-free, and with Henery Walker's five pounds too. "There's one thing," he ses to Bob; "you won't 'ave any of these other pore chaps money; and, if they're men, they ought to make it up to Henery Walker for the money he 'as saved 'em by finding you out."

"They've got to pay me fust," ses Bob. "I'm a pore man, but I'll stick up for my rights. As for me shooting 'em, they'd ha' been 'urt a good deal more if I'd done it—especially Mr. Henery Walker. Why, they're hardly 'urt at all."

"Don't answer 'im, Henery," ses John Biggs. "You save your breath to go and tell Sam Jones and the others about it. It'll cheer 'em up."

"And tell 'em about my arf, in case they get too cheerful and go overdoing it," ses Bob Pretty, stopping at the door. "Good-night all."

Nobody answered 'im; and arter waiting a little bit Henery Walker set off to see Sam Jones and the others. John Biggs was quite right about its making 'em cheerful, but they see as plain as Bob 'imself that it 'ad got to be kept quiet. "Till we've spent the money, at any rate," ses Walter Bell; "then p'r'aps Mr. Sutton might get Bob locked up for it."

Mr. Sutton went down to see 'em all a day or two afterwards. The shooting-party was broken up and gone 'ome, but they left some money behind 'em. Ten pounds each they was to 'ave, same as the others, but Mr. Sutton said that he 'ad heard 'ow the other money was wasted at the *Cauliflower,* and 'e was going to give it out to 'em ten shillings a week until the money was gorn. He 'ad to say it over and over agin afore they understood 'im, and Walter Bell 'ad to stuff the bedclo'es in 'is mouth to keep civil.

Peter Gubbins, with 'is arm tied up in a sling, was the fust one to turn up at the *Cauliflower,* and he was that down-'arted about it we couldn't do nothing with 'im. He 'ad expected to be able to pull out ten golden sovereigns, and the disapp'intment was too much for 'im.

"I wonder 'ow they heard about it," ses Dicky Weed.

"I can tell you," ses Bob Pretty, wot 'ad been sitting up in a corner by himself, nodding and smiling at Peter, wot wouldn't look at 'im. "A friend o' mine at Wickham wrote to him about it. He was so disgusted at the way Bill Chambers and Henery Walker come up 'ere wasting their 'ard-earned money, that he sent 'im a letter, signed 'A Friend of the Working Man,' telling 'im about it and advising 'im what to do."

"A friend o' yours?" ses John Biggs, staring at 'im. "What for?"

"I don't know," ses Bob; "he's a wunnerful good scholard, and he likes writin' letters. He's going to write another to-morrer, unless I go over and stop 'im."

"Another?" ses Peter, who 'ad been tellin' everybody that 'e wouldn't speak to 'im agin as long as he lived. "Wot about?"

"About the idea that I shot you all," ses Bob. "I want my character cleared. O' course, they can't prove anything against me—I've got my witnesses. But, taking one thing with another, I see now that it does look suspicious, and I don't suppose any of you'll get any more of your money. Mr. Sutton is so sick o' being laughed at, he'll jump at anything."

"You dursn't do it, Bob," ses Peter, all of a tremble.

"It ain't me, Peter, old pal," ses Bob, "it's my friend. But I don't mind stopping 'im for the sake of old times if I get my arf. He'd listen to me, I feel sure."

At fust Peter said he wouldn't get a farthing out of 'im if his friend wrote letters till Dooms-day; but by-and-by he thought better of it, and asked Bob to stay there while he went down to see Sam and Walter about it. When 'e came back he'd got the fust week's money for Bob Pretty; but he said he left Walter Bell carrying on like a madman, and, as for Sam Jones, he was that upset 'e didn't believe he'd last out the night.

W.W. Jacobs – A Short Biography

William Wymark Jacobs was born on September 8, 1863 in the Wapping district of London, England. An author, humorist and dramatist, Jacobs is best remembered for the enduring classic tale of horror - "The Monkey's Paw".

As a youth, Jacobs grew up near the Wapping docks in London, where his father was a wharf manager. The family's first home was home was a house on a River Thames wharf.

The docklands setting would show up frequently in his later literary output. Jacobs, the wharf rat, and his three siblings lost their mother when they were all still young children. Their father, William Gage Jacobs, remarried and fathered a further seven children with his erstwhile housekeeper Ellen Florey. Although he grew up surrounded by poverty, Jacobs himself received a formal education in London, first at a private prep school and later at the Birkbeck Literary and Scientific Institute (now part of the University of London and known as Birkbeck College).

Jacobs' adult working life began with a clerical position at the Post Office Savings Bank. The job was not a stimulating one but Jacobs put his imagination to good use and started to write short stories, sketches and articles, many of which appeared in the Post Office house publication "Blackfriars Magazine."

Although Jacobs did receive his fair share of rejection slips at the beginning of his career, many works written during this period of clerical employment appeared in the "Idler" and "Today" magazines, both of which were edited by noted humorist Jerome K. Jerome, who had taken a liking to Jacobs' stories.

From 1898, Jacobs also published stories in "The Strand", a popular, monthly fiction and general interest magazine. The arrangement stayed in place for most of his life and many of the works in Jacobs' subsequent collections – including the nautical serialization A Master of Craft (1899-1900) - appeared there first.

Jacobs' first volume of collected works was published in 1896. Many Cargoes, a selection of sea-faring yarns, established Jacobs as a popular writer and humorist with a penchant for authentic dialogue and trick endings (critics of the day referred to him as the "O. Henry of the Waterfront").

A year later he published a novelette, The Skipper's Wooing, and in 1898 another collection of short stories titled Sea Urchins. These works painted vivid, if imaginatively stretched, pictures of dockland and seafaring London with colourful characters (such as "The Night Watchman", Ginger Dick) that now seem archetypal.

Many of Jacobs' periodical publications and first editions were illustrated with woodcuts and ink drawings, as was still the custom at the turn of the 20th century. The author worked regularly with artists such as E.W. Kemble, who had illustrated Mark Twain's Adventures of Huckleberry Finn and Harriet Beecher Stowe's Uncle Tom's Cabin, and his good friend Will Owen, who eventually became a household name on the strength of his iconic Bisto Kids, Bovril and Lux Soap advertising posters.

By 1899, Jacobs was able to quit the post office and finally begin a career making a living as a full-time writer.

He married the noted suffragist Agnes Eleanor Williams (who had been jailed for her protest activities) in 1900. They set up a household in Loughton, Essex as well as living part of the year in central London. The couple went on to have five children together though their marriage was considered an unhappy one.

The publication of two short novels: At Sunwich Port (a romantic tale of rival sea captains in the fictional seaside community of Sunwich standing in for the actual East England community of

Sandwich, Kent) and Dialstone Lane (another small town romance involving intrigue and buried treasure), in 1902 and 1904 respectively, cemented Jacobs' reputation as one of the leading British authors of the new century.

On the foundations of a continuing ability to write for his audience he was readily published though he never strayed too far from what was becoming his familiar, dependable style. There followed a string of further successful publications, including Captain's All (1905), Night Watches (1914), The Castaways (1916), and Sea Whispers (1926). Jacobs published eighteen books in all during his lifetime; thirteen collections and five novels.

As a storyteller, Jacobs is perhaps better remembered for a handful of brief tales of the supernatural than for his popular nautical-themed works. The most famous of these, The Monkey's Paw, originally appeared as part of the 1902 short story collection The Lady of the Barge. It is an economically written story about a shriveled talisman, a monkey's paw that brings grief and horror in the wake of all too literal wish granting. The story has been adapted for other media repeatedly, starting with a one-act play performed at London's Haymarket Theatre in 1903. There have been multiple film adaptations of the story in the modern era; some of us are familiar with its appearance in an episode of the popular animated series, The Simpsons.

Another macabre gem, The Toll-House, was published as part of the collection Sailor's Knots in 1909. Jacob's once again employs a sparse style to tell the story of a group of men who spend the night in a famously haunted house on a dare (a noticeably similar narrative concept was put to use in the much earlier play The Ghost of Jerry Bundler, which had launched Jacobs' parallel career as a dramatist back in 1899 when it was produced at the St. James Theatre in London). Innovative at the time of writing, these sparingly written, atmospheric ghost stories are now familiar classics of the supernatural genre.

Though prolific in his younger years, Jacobs' productivity dropped dramatically after the start of World War I. Yet even in self-imposed semi-retirement Jacobs was still recognized as a leading humorist, ranked alongside such writers as P. G. Wodehouse and George Birmingham. He enjoyed continuing influence and elevated status among his fellow writers as evidenced by these comments attributed to his colleague Henry James:

"Mr. Jacobs, I envy you. You are popular! Your admirable work is appreciated by a wide circle of readers; it has achieved popularity. Mine never goes into a second edition."

James' literary fortunes would, of course, change, but his back-handedly complimentary admiration is compelling evidence of Jacobs' reputation as a writer and humourist both for his audience and his perhaps more admired literary colleagues.

Though Jacobs would create little in the way of new work after 1911, he was still writing. In these later years, seemingly burnt out creatively, Jacobs concentrated more on writing dramatizations and adaptations of his existing stories, including Beauty and the Barge (a film version starring Margaret Rutherford was also released in 1937) and In the Dark (a one act play that is often performed pr published with The Monkey's Paw adaptation).

Though admired by loyal readers throughout his lifetime, Jacobs has been almost completely forgotten since. Critics are at a loss to name a single reason why - Jacobs is universally considered to be a fine and imaginative literary craftsman. But, as critic John Wain suggested in a 1960 essay, perhaps Jacobs' humour may have been too gentle to persist into the cruel and sarcastic modern era, his dry pokes at proletariat hardship no longer suiting the times.

Nonetheless, Jacobs' legacy remains solid: he continued Dickens' (a writer with whom he is also often compared) tradition for sharing working class stories in authentic vernacular. And polished narratives such as The Monkey's Paw set a standard for the clever use of horror in fiction and popular culture that endures to this day. Indeed recently his works have begun to show an increased demand and appreciation in a world that is constantly looking over its shoulder.

William Wymark Jacobs died in a North London nursing home in Hornsey Lane, Islington on September 1st, 1943, just a week before his 80th birthday.

W.W. Jacobs – A Concise Bibliography

NOVELS AND SHORT STORY COLLECTIONS
MANY CARGOES (SHORT STORIES) (1896)
THE SKIPPER'S WOOING (1897)
SEA URCHINS (SHORT STORIES) (1898) aka MORE CARGOES
A MASTER OF CRAFT (1900)
LIGHT FREIGHTS (SHORT STORIES) (1901)
THE LADY OF THE BARGE (SHORT STORIES) (1902)
AT SUNWICH PORT (1902)
DIALSTONE LANE (1902)
SALTHAVEN (1908)
CAPTAINS ALL (SHORT STORIES) (1911)
NIGHT WATCHERS (SHORT STORIES) (1914)
DEEP WATERS (SHORT STORIES) (1919)

SHORT STORIES (INCLUDING THOSE USED IN THE COLLECTIONS ABOVE)
A BENEFIT PERFORMANCE
A BLACK AFFAIR
A CASE OF DESERTION
A CHANGE OF TREATMENT
A CIRCULAR TOUR
A DISCIPLINARIAN
A DISTANT RELATIVE
A GARDEN PLOT
A GOLDEN VENTURE
A HARBOUR OF REFUGE
A LOVE KNOT
A LOVE PASSAGE
A MARKED MAN
A MIXED PROPOSAL
A RASH EXPERIMENT
A SAFETY MATCH
A SPIRIT OF AVARICE
A TIGER'S SKIN
ADMIRAL PETERS
AFTER THE INQUEST
ALF'S DREAM

THE SUBSTITUTE
THE TEMPTATION OF SAMUEL BURGE
THE TEST
THE THREE SISTERS
TO HAVE AND TO HOLD
"THE TOLL-HOUSE"
TWIN SPIRITS
TWO OF A TRADE
THE UNDERSTUDY
THE UNKNOWN
THE VIGIL
WATCH-DOGS
THE WEAKER VESSEL
THE WELL
THE WHITE CAT

STAGE
THE GHOST OF JERRY BUNDLER (1899) (In London)

FILM ADAPTATIONS
A MASTER OF CRAFT (1922)
THE MONKEY'S PAW (1933)
OUR RELATIONS, a Laurel & Hardy film, "suggested by" to Jacobs' "The Money Box." (1936)
FOOTSTEPS IN THE FOG, from the short story The Interruption. (1955)